# FROM THE ADVENTURES OF SAILOR TOM SHARKEY

I HAD THROWN a variety of my best rights and lefts, the likes of which would have taken anyone else's head off, had they landed. However, those big, pin-wheeling arms kept rotating and knocking my fists out of the air even as I was counterpunching. I felt like a flat-footed dub fighting this scrap metal monkey, and it was irritating me more than somewhat.

I backed off, my arms numb to the elbow from hitting the I-beams this thing had for wrists. No sooner did I put my guard back up when that monster's long, slicing left actually looped around my gloves and caught me in the side of the head.

I dropped to the ground with a bunch of Chinese gongs going off in my ears. What a punch! It felt just like getting hit by a horseshoe thrown by an elephant. I got up quickly, but the robot had backed off.

The crowd was laughing and clapping like they'd just seen a show. Cain was talking again, but I couldn't hear him for the ringing in my ears and the roaring fighting Irish blood surging through me. I wasn't going to be made a fool of, not by some scrap metal monkey...

# The Adventures of
# SAILOR TOM SHARKEY

A COLLECTION OF
TWO-FISTED
FIGHT CARD STORIES

# MARK FINN

2014
F**I**GHTCARD

FIGHT CARD: THE ADVENTURES OF SAILOR TOM SHARKEY

e-Book Edition – First Published June 2014

Paperback Edition Published June 2014

Copyright © 2014 Mark Finn

Cover by Carl Yonder © 2014

This is a work of fiction. Characters, corporations, institutions and organizations mentioned in this novel are either the product of the author's imagination or, if real, used fictitiously without any intent to describe actual conduct.

All rights reserved. No part of this book may be reproduced or transmitted in any form or by any means, electronic or mechanical, including photocopying, recording or by any information storage and retrieval system, without prior permission from the publisher.

# TABLE OF CONTENTS

| | |
|---|---|
| Introduction: Sailor Tom Sharkey – A Literary History | 1 |
| Sailor Tom Sharkey and the Induction Window | 11 |
| Sailor Tom Sharkey and the Real McCoy | 25 |
| Sailor Tom Sharkey and the Tinseltown Terror | 37 |
| Sailor Tom Sharkey and the Electric Gorilla | 51 |
| Sailor Tom Sharkey and the Phantom of the Gentleman Farmer's Commune | 69 |
| Sailor Tom Sharkey and the South Seas Cormorant | 81 |
| Sailor Tom Sharkey and the Christmas Savages | 95 |

# SAILOR TOM SHARKEY
# A LITERARY HISTORY

THERE ARE PERHAPS two dozen well-known boxing stories of substance, ranging from Jack London's *A Piece of Steak*, and *Fifty Grand* by Ernest Hemingway, to more popular fare, such as sports writer Damon Runyan's *Bred for Battle* and P.G. Wodehouse's *The Debut of Battling Billson*. More recent stories by Rick Bass' *The Legend of Pig-Eye* and Thom Jones' *Sonny Liston Was a Friend of Mine* would surely be included, as well. Anyone wishing to expand the list to include novels would have some classic fare to choose from: Harold Robbins' *A Stone for Danny Fisher* instantly springs to mind, along with the excellent book, *The Bruiser* by actual boxer-turned-author Jim Tully. There are a lot of boxing stories out there, along with boxing fans who are writers of one stripe or another; from Alexandre Dumas to Arthur Conan Doyle, from Norman Mailer to Joyce Carol Oates, it's easy to find books waxing rhapsodic about *the Sweet Science* as literature, as metaphor, or as simply a cracking good read.

And yet, there is one name always missing from the Table of Contents pages of the *Best Boxing Stories of Forever and All Time (Until We Make Another Book Just Like This One)* and that's Robert E. Howard. Most people know him, if at all, as the creator of Conan the Barbarian. They may know that he was a Texan, who wrote a bunch of pulp fiction stories in Cross Plains, Texas in the 1920s and 1930s for magazines like the legendary *Weird Tales*. If they know anything else, it's that he died young, at the age of 30, by his own hand.

They almost never know he wrote over sixty boxing stories from 1926 to 1936, including some poetry, which were his bread and butter during his early writing career. Most of the stories centered on Sailor Steve Costigan, a *ham and egg* fighter sailing on the merchant marine *Sea Girl*. He – and some of his other, later fictional brothers – spent their days in the ports of call in the Asiatic Seas. They scrapped to survive, for the honor of a beautiful girl, or for a fellow sailor in trouble. Full of humor, incredible boxing sequences, and double and triple crosses, all told from the point of view of Sailor Steve himself, one of the most unreliable narrators to ever grace the page. Howard also wrote some serious boxing stories, such as the novella *The Iron Man*, but his meat and potatoes were found in these bawdy burlesque boxing stories.

Howard was a lifelong boxing enthusiast. He read about it, he wrote about it – hell, he nearly lived it. Himself an amateur boxer, Howard participated in a number of both gloved and bare-knuckle matches with the local roughnecks in his home town of Cross Plains. He wrote about these fights, and traveled far and wide to see local and regional matches and exhibitions. Howard even wrote a number of unfinished essays to gather his thoughts on boxing into one place. These thoughts, these ideas of Howard, while unfinished and unpublished in his lifetime, ended up elsewhere, hidden deep in his fiction as a primary motivating influence.

When I first encountered Howard's boxing stories, I knew none of this. I was just a fan of the Texas author's work. I'd read Conan, of course, and his other hero-kings, Bran Mak Morn, and King Kull. I was familiar with some of his other heroic writings, but I'd never seen any of his boxing stories before. The book was *The Incredible Adventures of Dennis Dorgan*. On the cover was a stereotypical *evil oriental* – a Fu Manchu villain straight from Central Casting. This was modern-day fare by way of the 1920's.

Intrigued, I bought the book and took it home.

The first story I read wasn't the first story in the book. Instead, I skipped right over to *The Destiny Gorilla*, a title I maintain to this day is technically perfect for so many reasons. As soon as I started reading the story, I knew I was in uncharted waters. Gone was the florid, compact language of Howard's dark fantasy stories. This was light, wide-open, riddled with dialect and malapropisms, and really funny dialogue. I started laughing, and I laughed all the way through the story.

I was still laughing when my roommate and fellow Howard fan came home. He put up with me for about fifteen minutes, and then demanded to know what I was doing. I gave him the book, and within two pages, he was laughing, too. We spent the rest of the evening wondering out loud why we'd never seen any of this before now. That night, we both became lifelong fans of Howard's boxing stories. And we weren't even reading the best of his boxing work.

Years later, when I starting looking seriously at studying and writing about Robert E. Howard, I joined what was then ground zero for such folks, REHUPA – an amateur press association that stands for the Robert E. Howard United Press Association.

When I joined, I expected to be the only person interested in the boxing stories. I was wrong. There were two others: Leo Grin and Chris Gruber. Both had come to the boxing material, just as I had, and come to the same conclusion as me – why didn't more people know about this? In fact, we all joined with the idea of cracking open the boxing stories and showing these other Howard fans what was what.

We banded together, and right from the start, we began elevating each other's work. There were conversations, revelations, shared information...it was heady stuff. We were the outcasts among the outcasts, writing with something to prove. We knew this stuff was great. We just had to show other people.

One of the areas of interest we shared was in sifting through Howard's work to find his influences. His unpublished essays and stories were invaluable in this area. Chris Gruber's essay, *Atavists, All?*, was a lightning rod pointing to Howard's utilization of the kind of throw-back boxer he admired, first mentioned in the unpublished essay *Men of Iron*, was the model for every single Howard character in his heroic fiction canon.

Boom!

While pouring through the names of boxers in *Men of Iron*, Leo wrote a huge essay about Joe Grimm, who was prominently mentioned in essay. I became enamored with another real-life golden age boxer listed alongside of Grimm – *Sailor Tom Sharkey*. I don't know what it was about the name, or maybe it was the story Howard included in the essay about Sharkey being knocked out of the ring on his head, and getting up to finish the fight, that intrigued me, but something took hold, and I began to research Tom Sharkey in earnest.

There was very little online about Sharkey, the most substantial piece being a biographical sketch by boxing expert Tracey Callis, alongside of his ring record. I had some boxing reference books in my personal library already, including a great encyclopedia from *The Ring*, the Bible of boxing, and a magazine Howard read regularly in his day. Inside was an amazing picture of Tom Sharkey, after a fight, standing straight and tall, like he was having a mug shot taken. He was battered, crunched, and bruised, but everything I could see in his curiously shaped head and face and thick-as-a-bull neck made me proclaim, "Tom Sharkey, hell, that's Sailor Steve Costigan!"

And thus began my quest. I chased down every scrap of information I could find about Sharkey. He was one of the most feared and respected boxers in the Golden Age of the sport – just after the reign of John L. Sullivan.

Sharkey trod the *squared circle* with the likes of Gentleman Jim Corbett, Bob Fitzsimmons, and – perhaps his greatest nemesis – Jim Jeffries. These were some of the biggest, hardest hitting fighters of all time. And they all said Sailor Tom Sharkey gave them their toughest fights.

Standing only 5'8" or 5'9" depending on who you ask, Sharkey had a 46" chest and thick, muscled arms he honed from his years at sea in the merchant marine, and later, the U.S. Navy. Born in Dundalk, Ireland, in 1874, he ran away at the age of 12, and managed to make it all the way to America as a sailor by the time he was 17. He traded briefly as a blacksmith before signing on to a hitch in the Navy. When he arrived in San Francisco, two years later, he was ready to begin his fighting career in earnest.

Because of his size, and his Irish accent, no one took him very seriously at first. Even then, there was a frequently debunked myth that all sailors were decent brawlers, but against an actual student of boxing, stood little chance. Sharkey wasn't the best public speaker, and he looked like a dub – his chest, for example, was festooned with a tattoo of a four-masted schooner and the motto, *Never Give Up the Ship*. He was Popeye twenty years before E.C. Segar created *Thimble Theater*.

Sharkey's initial matches were literally intended to be good sport for better boxers and nothing else. But Sharkey surprised them all when he charged the local champions and kept them on the run for eight straight rounds. He could absorb massive amounts of punishment, and his punch was devastating. Early opponents learned this the hard way after waking up on the canvas, wondering what hit them. Sharkey quickly rose through the ranks to become a contender in San Francisco. He had his eye set on the heavyweight championship.

His professional career was as controversial as it was colorful and storied. Sharkey wasn't so much a fighter as he was a force of nature. His preferred method of boxing was to come out swinging and not stop until his opponent was down. He didn't mind taking a few punches in order to get in close with those tree trunk arms and that fireplug torso and whale away on the other guy's ribcage – and if a couple of kidney punches landed, too, well, no hard feelings, eh?

Not quite. Fouls, low blows, and other controversies dogged Sharkey and made other opponents wary of stepping into the ring with the Irish scrapper. His reputation notwithstanding, Sharkey tried several times to wrest the belt from champions, only to end in bitter defeat. One of his most bizarre fights was against lanky Bob Fitzsimmons, another blacksmith-turned-boxer whose punch was legendary, despite his unassuming appearance.

The match, refereed by none other than Wild West lawman Wyatt Earp, was awarded to Fitzsimmons because of a low blow thrown by Sharkey that Earp observed. The incident actually ended up on court, with Sharkey alleging Fitzsimmons faked the injury because he knew Sharkey would beat him. The judge abided by the decision, and Sharkey never got a rematch with Fitz.

But the most storied battles of Sharkey's career were his two brutal fights with Jim Jeffries. The second fight, in particular, is the stuff of legend. It was the first boxing match filmed and shown in movie theaters. The Klieg lights used to illuminate the ring were so bright and intense that it singed both men's scalps. Sharkey fought Jeffries to a standstill in 25 grueling rounds that nearly did both boxers in. Sharkey fought the last four rounds with three broken ribs. He was certain he'd beat Jeffries, but the referee didn't agree. Afterwards, even on the mend, Sharkey threatened to throw the ref into the Atlantic Ocean if he ever caught up with him.

Sharkey's post boxing career was just as colorful, and involved him opening clubs, getting embroiled in Tammany Hall politics in New York City, betting large sums of money on the horses, getting married twice, widowed once, and divorced once, and later, in his fifties, going on the Vaudeville Circuit with former nemesis Jim Jeffries and recounting their famous fights for the crowds.

Sharkey loved to spin yarns, and some of those he told people over the years were colorful and, um, hard to prove, such as the notion he was shipwrecked four times in the Merchant Marine. Over the years, sports writers, reporters, and fellow boxers had amusing Tom Sharkey stories to tell. Most are affectionate in their good humor. Some are just downright funny.

These anecdotes and snippets were all published during the time Robert E. Howard was reading about boxing. I was certain I'd found the framework upon which he built Sailor Steve Costigan. These findings and essays made their way into various books, introductions, and lectures.

By this time, I'd corresponded with most of the people who had written anything about Tom Sharkey, including the author of the first real biography of the man, *I Fought Them All: the Life and Ring Battles of Prizefighting Legend Tom Sharkey*, Greg Lewis. To a person, they were all happy to share in their research and enthusiasm for this colorful fighter.

At this point, I'd been engaged in this pursuit, on and off, for five or six years. As my file on Tom Sharkey grew ever larger, and my parallel study of Howard's boxing went ever deeper, I felt an urge to write some funny boxing stories of my own start to take hold in my brain.

This was folly, of course, and I'll tell you why. It has been scientifically proven over the years that one cannot copy the writing style of Robert E. Howard. It just can't be done, and we know this, because it was tried...a lot...with terrible, terrible results.

Howard's writing style was literary lighting in a bottle. It was alchemy. Mercurial. It can be imitated, to some degree, but it can never be duplicated. The reason for this is simple – no one writes from the head space from which Howard wrote. His work was very personal, and unless you have the exact same set of interests, pressures, and irritants, you'll never make pearls the way Howard made them.

Add to that the fact that doing a Sailor Steve Costigan story involved writing funny, and you'll see the task is nigh-impossible. Writing in someone else's humor style is even harder than writing in someone else's literary style, and if you tried to do a Sailor Steve Costigan story, you'd have to do both. I'm no fool. Whatever marginal cache I had as a Howardist would be shattered if I tried to write something *in the style of Robert E. Howard*, a practice I'd publically pooh-poohed many times.

No, if I was going to do a humorous boxing story, it would have to be original. My own thing. I knew I could write about the fights, and I was pretty sure I could make it funny in my particular way, but I was floundering as to what this boxer would look like, and how he'd actually be different from Sailor Steve.

The inspiration came to me during a writer's retreat in 2007. My former writing group and publishing consortium, Clockwork Storybook, got together at Naulakha, Rudyard Kipling's house in Dummerston, Vermont, and we spent a week in seclusion, writing and critiquing, just like the old days.

Literally three days before we were set to meet up, it occurred to me there was no better unreliable narrator than Tom Sharkey himself. He went around the world, did all of these amazing things, and like any old campaigner worth his salt, wasn't going to let the truth get in the way of a good story.

There were a lot of "blank spaces" on Tom Sharkey's map – periods of time no one can account for, including the years he spent with a traveling carnival, recreating (and sometimes rehashing, at the age of fifty, no less) his fights with Jim Jeffries.

I wrote the first Tom Sharkey story – what would become *Sailor Tom Sharkey and the Introduction Window* (the original title was *An Excerpt from the Unexpurgated Adventures of Sailor Tom Sharkey*) – right before I left for Vermont.

I planned to read it for the guys, and get their notes. During the retreat, I wrote another story based on a writing challenge we all set for ourselves. This one, *The Final Adventure of Sailor Tom Sharkey*, has since been renamed *Sailor Tom Sharkey and the Real McCoy*. It has also been edited and rewritten somewhat to strip out most of the challenge conditions of the exercise. I kept the cow skull, though, which worked out quite well.

When I read the group my first Tom Sharkey story, it was with very little preamble. I just told them this was something I'd been working up to for a while. To my complete surprise and pleasure, they loved it. Most of the comments were along the lines of, "I can't tell if this is good writing from you or not, because it sounds just like you." The second story, written a few days into the retreat, met with similar notes and a caution to be careful not to have them all sound alike. "I mean, how often can you write about a big dumb sailor who doesn't ever get what's going on around him?" one of them quipped. Oh, ye of little faith.

Other Tom Sharkey stories began to suggest themselves, and I dutifully noted them down when inspiration struck. The hardest part of writing Tom Sharkey is avoiding "Costigan Creep," when certain key phrases and things find their way, in quantity, into the stories. Do it once and it's a nice little Easter egg nod to fans in the know. Do it twice, or thrice, and then it becomes second-rate Robert E. Howard. More than once I've had to pull myself back, all in service to the story.

I should also mention that over the span of several years and several stories, my fictitious Sailor Tom Sharkey has taken on a life of his own, one that is suggested by the real fighter, but has in the retelling become someone else altogether.

I've based many of these stories on real events in Sharkey's life, but these are in no way intended to represent real people or real events, and none of the stories in this collection are intended to supplant the real Tom Sharkey's biography in any way. If you want the details of the man behind the legends, see Greg Lewis' book, mentioned above.

In between writing other things, I'd occasionally let one fly, and when finished, I sent each one far and wide, looking for a home. They were, not surprisingly, hard to place. There is not, nor has there ever been, a sub-genre of the literature section labeled "humorous historical weird boxing stories." An oversight, no doubt.

My submissions, to editors of big and little stature, all came back rejected. Those that added any commentary frequently told me they liked the story, but had no idea what to do with it. I wasn't surprised. These have been a hard sell.

And yet, every time I write a new Tom Sharkey story, and

read it at conventions or other personal appearances, I get laughs and interest. "When are you going to collect these?" "Where can I read more?"

Thank heaven for Fight Card. Now, at last, you can.

I'm grateful to Paul Bishop for giving me the chance to publish this collection under the aegis of what has become a respected line of quality fight fiction, and ground zero for fans of this kind of literature. If you are such a fan (and why wouldn't you be?) and you have not read Robert E. Howard's boxing stories, you really need to. You're missing out on one of the most memorable and critically underrated achievements from one of the world's greatest pulp fiction writers. If you're already one of us, then I hope you'll enjoy these stories in the spirit in which I wrote them.

Mark Finn
June 2014

# SAILOR TOM SHARKEY AND THE INDUCTION WINDOW

SOME OF THE BEST times I had was all of the years I toured the country with the Lawrence Julius Cavalcade of Super Stars Vaudeville show. I got to see this beautiful country of ours two or three times, and let me tell you, it's worth seeing. I had a great time doing shows with Jim Jeffries and we spent many hours sparring and recalling the various tales of our misspent youth. Jeff became a good friend to me, and it was in no small part due to this one time we was passing through Texas.

It was during my second continental tour, and we were on our way to El Paso, having missed it the first time around. The train was in bad shape, because boss man Larry was tight with a nickel, and we had to pull into a small town called Marfa to take on water.

The conductor was this nervous Irish guy named O'Herling, and he called Larry over to tell him everything that was wrong with the engine, which is what he did every time the train started or stopped. This time, though, it looked like we were going to be stopped a while. So, Jeff and I got off the train with the Ling family and Stumpy the goon, and we all went into town for an ice cream soda.

We musta looked funny going down the street – two pug-ugly ex-boxers, a dog-faced imbecile, and twelve Chinamen of various sizes, all strolling down the street like it was New Year's Eve in Brooklyn or something. A few of the fellows in town recognized Jeff, and a couple of them even recognized me, and once we signed a few autographs and explained what we were doing, they stopped throwing rocks at Stumpy and let us be on our way.

At the drugstore, we all piled in and Jeff ordered ice cream for everyone, him being pretty generous with his poker winnings. He also knew if Ling Soo tried to order ice cream for his family, Ling Soo would just muck it up and we'd have to punch our way out of town like we did in Estes Park last year – I never saw such a dust-up over the word *vanirra* in my life.

Some folks ain't too tolerant of Chinese people. Me, I've always liked 'em. Especially the Ling family. They're good eggs, and besides, grandma Ling is a whiz at five card draw.

So, Jeff and I sorta stood guard while they ate and browsed the newsstand. I had Jeff read me the latest news from *The Ring* and we laughed at what Dempsey was up to in the society pages. It was about that time this tall, thin, wild-haired looking fellow with goggles strapped to his head burst in the door.

He breezed right by us, muttering, "A gorilla and a grizzly, a gorilla and a grizzly," in some sort of funny accent.

He ran down the length of the counter and then he caught sight of the two of us and hurried over, intent on making our acquaintance. The skinny fellow says, "Are you Jim Jefferies and Sailor Tom Sharkey?"

Yeah, we reply.

The man stuck out his hand. "Viktor Nachenblitzen."

I shook hands, cautiously, because there was something dangerous in the guy's demeanor. He was like the cobras Rama Singh, our fake Indian swami, handled from time to time. I didn't trust the Nachen-whatever fellow for a second.

Nachenblitzen shook Jeff's hand and then he said, "I've just been to the train station, where your manager, Mister Julius, and I, have made...an arrangement." He smiled apologetically. "Your train, it seems, needs some repairs. In addition to my other various talents, I am proficient in the workings of steam engines. Therefore, I have agreed to make the repairs to your train, *gratis*, if I could have some assistance this evening for a series of experiments I plan to conduct out in the hills on the outside of town." He made a vague sweeping motion behind him toward nothing I could see. "My equipment is considerable and heavy, but I am sure that given your impressive stature, you could make short work of it."

Jeff, I could tell, was fixing to say yes, but I stopped him. "Listen, Pal, I don't think you know who you're talking to, here. This is Jim Jefferies, former heavyweight champion of the world."

"Indeed?" said Nachenblitzen. "Are you Mister Jeffries' solicitor?"

"It don't matter if I'm the king of Siam. Neither one of us is anyone else's porter." Jeff put a hand on my shoulder, but I waved him off. "No, Jeff, I'm serious. Go hire some Mexicans or something. There's about a million of 'em around here."

"Well, yes," said Nachenblitzen, "but you see, this is ranching country, and everyone who could help me is out working the cattle. Besides," he said, his face darkening, "I am not entirely certain I would trust them with my equipment. Some of the instruments are extremely delicate."

"There you go," I said. "You don't want us hauling your junk around. We're boxers. We don't know nothing about no delicate instruments."

"Well, gentlemen, I am sorry to have wasted your time," he said, turning away. "I had rather hoped, given your fame and stature, you would naturally be interested in my work…"

I watched him walk toward the door, wondering if he was serious about me being made into a statue. Maybe he was on to something, after all. "Say, what kind of experiments are you running, anyway?"

Nachenblitzen turned around, his eyes twinkling. "Have you ever heard of ball lightning?" he asked.

"Nope. I didn't know lightning had hair."

He laughed, and so did Jeff. Then he started telling me about quartz rocks and lighting and something about the temperature of the earth and all kinds of stuff I've forgotten since. But the funny thing is, the more he talked about it, the more interesting it sounded. He also said if his experiment was a success there would be newspaper stories written about it, and naturally, he would have to mention his two helpers.

When he put it that way – that we'd be helping him to invent electricity or something – then it all made good promotional sense for the show that we should be on hand.

Nachenblitzen pulled us outside to where he'd parked a beat-up old truck and showed us a bunch of consoles with dials, and some weird-looking towers with balls on the end, and before we knew what was happening, we both agreed to help him later that day.

So, we walked Stumpy and the Lings back to the train and stood around for a while, letting the locals gawk at us and signing a few autographs. Some of the other performers got off the train and were doing their acts for the crowd as they passed the hat around.

Jeff didn't want to spar none, and I was getting antsy just standing around like a rube, so I helped Smitty and Calvin load wood and coal onto the train for a while. That seemed to calm my nerves a bit.

I don't know why I was so jumpy. Maybe it was because I felt like Nachenblitzen had tricked me into helping him. I asked Jeff about it, and he said I was just imagining things. I told him that wasn't the case, and he said it was, and I called him a liar, and before you know it, we were sparring despite what Jeff wanted.

Afterward, we changed out of our ruined traveling duds and into something more suitable for hard labor. I put on my dungarees and an undershirt and a work shirt, taking it easy because Jeff had cracked a couple of ribs while everyone hooted and hollered outside the train.

Jeff broke out a pair of his farming overalls and a big straw hat, which made everyone laugh. He had a certain way about him that made everyone like him. I never got that way. I was always glad to meet people, but people weren't always glad to meet me.

By noon, the Texas heat was killing us. We sat around in the available shade, drinking ice water we'd snitched from the dining car, until Nachenblitzen drove up in his big red truck full of junk, which was all under a couple of tarps.

One of the tarps was covered in these big, impressive words. Jeff read 'em aloud, "Professor V. Nachenblitzen, Master of Lightning, Lord of Electricity, Purveyor of Modern Medicinal Wonders." I asked Jeff to tell me what the hell it all meant, and he said it meant this guy was a flim-flam man.

Nachenblitzen jumped out of the cab and had a quick conversation with Larry. He then walked over to us and said, "Gentlemen, are we ready?"

I threw a murderous look at Larry, who caught it on the chin and then pretended to be very interested in what else was wrong with the engine. I suppose I could have refused to help Nachenblitzen, which would fix Larry, but it also would have messed up the rest of the show if we couldn't get to El Paso on time.

Anyway, I was bored stiff. Besides, Jeff was going, and we were kind of paired up as a set. So, I shrugged my shoulders and made for to go.

It was crowded in the cab of the truck. We all managed to all pile in, but I had to shift gears for Nachenblitzen when he told me. That was uncomfortable. Especially second gear.

To add insult to injury, Nachenblitzen wasn't the world's greatest driver, neither. Two or three times, he swerved and veered away from a ditch we'd been about to crash into and every time he'd get back on the road, flushed red with embarrassment, and mumble an apology.

Finally, I caught him looking at me out of the corner of his eye. He looked away real fast, and we swerved again, and I lost my temper at him. I said, "What's so goddamn fascinatin' about me that you keep trying to kill us?"

Nachenblitzen kinda turtled down into his collar and apologized again. We drove in silence for a couple of minutes, and then Nachenblitzen asked, like he was changing the subject or something, "May I ask what happened to your ear?"

I started laughing, and then Jeff started laughing, and then Nachenblitzen started laughing, even though it was pretty clear he didn't know what he was laughing at.

So, I told him how I got my cauliflowers and that reminded Jeff about the first fight we had, and then we started telling Nachenblitzen stories of our ring exploits, in earnest.

I thought at first Nachenblitzen was going to faint from our discussion of various injuries inflicted upon us by well-meaning adversaries, but as it turns out, he was pretty interested, and kept asking questions. Jeff had to answer most of them since Nachenblitzen wanted to know stuff like timing counter-punches and all of that nonsense I never bothered with when I was boxing.

After a little backtracking, we found the trail leading out into the mountains. It was slow going, because of how loaded down the truck was, and by the time we reached Nachenblitzen's campsite, we were all drenched with sweat and glad to be out of the cab where we could catch the breeze that blew through the hills every so often.

Nachenblitzen had set up about a hundred yards from the edge of a couple of shallow canyons that fed down into a creek bed in a sort of rough half circle on either side. There was a trail leading down to the creek, which had water in it, but I could also see a number of red flags planted about halfway up the side of each hill. Jeff saw it too, and we took turns wondering what the flags were for, when Nachenblitzen came over and told us it was where his little towers were going to go.

It was tough work, and I'm not kidding. I felt like I was back at sea again. Jeff and I would haul out a tower, which was about three feet tall and heavy – made out of iron and wood with a weird-looking ball on the end – and carry it out to the hillside.

We had to be careful because there wasn't any trail, and several times we slipped and skidded down the slope with Nachenblitzen hollering for us to shield the tower with our bodies.

We'd get to where a flag was, and Nachenblitzen would come out with a coil of wire and a wooden box. While we sorta buried the tower into the ground a ways, Nachenblitzen would attach some of the wire to the underside of the weird-looking ball. Then we'd go get another tower while he wrote down numbers in a notebook, muttering in some foreign language.

It was sunset by the time we finished. The whole set-up looked like the Chicago World's Fair, with silver towers gleaming in the sun and wires strung every which way, including over the creek and back again. I thought it looked pretty neat, and so did Jeff.

Nachenblitzen passed out a few canteens of water and some sandwiches he'd bought from the diner in town. We wolfed all of that down and then Jeff and I passed my flask back and forth until it was gone.

Meanwhile, Nachenblitzen hooked up the wires from the towers into a couple of big metal consoles that were so heavy we didn't even bother to take down off of the truck. Finally, he jumped down and ran halfway back up the left side hill. He pulled a long stick out of the ground and looked at it carefully, and then he shouted back at us, "Eighty-six degrees Fahrenheit, gentlemen! It's about to start!"

He ran back over to us and as the daylight slowly fell behind the mountains, Nachenblitzen put on his goggles and motioned us over. I asked him, "So, what's all of this stuff for, anyway, Vic?"

"I'm creating an induction field, Mister Sharkey," he said.

"I don't need to meet the field," I told him. "I've been tramping all over it for the past five hours. Me and this field are on a first name basis."

Nachenblitzen laughed again, and so did Jeff. I couldn't see what was so funny, because I didn't understand a word that came out of Nachenblitzen's mouth. But he was excited about it, and that kinda made us excited, too.

The consoles in front of Nachenblitzen started humming, and the dials started spinning, and some lights came on, dim at first, but then they got brighter and brighter. Nachenblitzen was so happy, he was jumping up and down in the truck bed. "It's working! I can't believe it! It's working!" he said, over and over.

Jeff nudged me and I glanced over to where he was pointing and saw the most curious and impressive thing I've ever seen in my life. The balls on all of the little towers we'd planted were glowing white-hot, and there was electricity racing around the wire that we could see, in waves, like ripples in water. Inside the circle of wire that ran over the hills, everything was blue and hazy.

"Well, I ain't no scientist or nothing like that, but that's pretty weird," I said, and Jeff agreed with me.

I looked over at Nachenblitzen to get our observation confirmed, but he was too busy watching the sky above the two hills. "Ahoy, Vic! You seeing this?" I yelled over the increasing hum.

"Ya, ya," he said, waving at me, his eyes never leaving the sky above the hills. "Keep an eye on the field and tell me what it's doing!"

With all of this interesting stuff happening in the valley, and Nachenblitzen more interested in the skies above, I was beginning to think maybe he wasn't too tightly wrapped, if you take my meaning.

Then Jeff saw something and elbowed me in my cracked ribs so hard that it knocked the breath out of me. Riding into the creek was a whole passel of Mexican banditos, pistols cracking and everyone cussing to beat the bishop.

Jeff and I immediately dove flat so they wouldn't see us, and we got another surprise. From the ground, we could see the creek bed on the other side, and damned if it wasn't empty and quiet and free of Mexicans on horseback.

I stood up and looked through the blue window again, and there they all were, being chased by U.S. Calvary. Staring into that racing blue electrical field, it was just like watching a moving picture show.

I told Jeff it was okay to stand up and watch the show, but no sooner than he stood up, a bullet whizzed past my ear and embedded itself into the back of one of Nachenblitz's consoles.

I looked around to see who in the hell was shooting at us and caught a glimpse of Nachenblitzen spinning dials and flipping levers like he was driving a submarine. When I didn't see anyone in our immediate vicinity, I looked back at Jeff, but he was busy staring into the blue window again.

This time, the creek was full of water, and all of the Mexican bandits and cavalry men were gone. Instead, the creek floor was full of Indians. I have to say, I met some of the Indians in Bill Cody's Wild West Show, and these fellows didn't look nothing like the ones I met. It was like the difference between seeing a picture of a lion and then going to the circus and seeing one in person.

They were celebrating for doing something, dancing and laughing as their horses drank water. One of them threw his axe up and I watched it break the surface of the blue window before falling back down to the ground.

Jeff said something about what an arm that guy had, and I noticed two things. One is that they were all looking at us. Two is that the blue window, which used to be inside the wires, was now outside of the wires and slowly climbing up the hillside.

"Nachenblitzen!" I shouted above the loud humming, "look at yer interduction field!"

I heard Nachenblitzen say, "Well, that's not right...!" and then the field flickered again. Now the creek bed had become a river with funny looking trees along the sides. And the hills weren't scrub grass no more, neither, but long, spade-like leaves like jungle plants or something. Jeff and I peered down into the blue field again, straining for evidence of the cowboys and Indians. That's when something splashed into the water. It was hot, because it made a lot of steam when it hit. More things were falling out of the sky, thudding into the hillsides and sending up a spray of rocks.

Then something huge fell, and for a second, it looked like a weird-looking rock, and before we could do anything, there were rocks and water spewing into the air through the blue window. Some of the rocks hit me, but it was only a glancing blow to my head, so that wasn't an injury worth mentioning. Jeff hit me harder than that in practice. Oh, yeah, and the blue window was growing again, faster than before.

I hollered to Nachenblitzen, but he was already ahead of me. He turned some more dials, and everything flickered again, and all at once, the stream was free of falling rocks. It looked like Nachenblitzen was finally getting the hang of the machine, but when I looked again, the field was now almost at our feet. I got the distinct impression that this was not good.

Just then, a group of animals came wandering down the edge of the river, drinking the water. They were the weirdest-looking lizards I ever seen, and they were as big as a horse, easy. Kinda without meaning to, I said, "What the hell are those things?"

Jeff later told me they were dinosaurs. There was a picture in a book and he called them a Para-sail-opolis or something like that. He's a lot smarter than me in all kinds of ways. He does have a farm, after all, so he'd know a lot more about animals than a dub like me. I just called them hornheads because of that stupid-looking backward horn sticking out of their forehead.

Anyway, I thought the hornhead dinosaurs heard me because they jumped like they'd been kicked. And that's when we heard this deep, rattling scream, and another dinosaur jumped down the slope of the far hill. It was much bigger than the other dinosaurs; like two or three of Nachenblitzen's red trucks, all thrown together. It was nothing but teeth and claws and it landed on one of the smaller dinosaurs and we heard the bones snap.

Jeff called that one Al O'Saurus. I don't know how Jeff came to be on a first name basis with the dinosaurs, but there you go. Figures that this big lug would be Irish. Always hungry and always fighting. I rubbed my ribs, knowing the feeling. Al roared and threw his head back, and I'm telling you the god's honest truth, he saw us standing at the top of the hill, gawking at him.

I realized a number of things all at once. Number one, that blue field we were staring into wasn't no moving picture screen. It was more like a window. An open window.

Number two, I was pretty sure that, as tired as I was, I could run back to town faster than Nachenblitzen could drive that truck.

Number three, there weren't but about a dozen steps for that monster before he'd be up to where we were, and that would present an entirely new and unique situation for someone like myself.

"Vic!" I bellowed. "We got trouble here!"

"What?" he yelled back. I tried to point it out to him, but his eyes widened and he ducked down behind his equipment. I turned around and saw that I was right in the path of the stampeding hornheads who were scrambling up the slope of the hill, trying to put as much distance between Al and themselves as possible.

Well, I couldn't let Nachenblitzen get trampled by these things, so I squared off and took aim at the lead hornhead and as soon as it got close enough that I could see the panic in its eyes, I cranked back my left and threw an overhead smash into the bridge of its cow-like nose. It honked in surprise and reared back on its hind legs, which brought the rest of them skidding to a stop at the edge of the hill.

It ducked its goofy looking head down and tried to ram me, but I was ready for it and pivoted out of the way. That gave me a great handle to get the hornhead into a headlock, and as there was no referees around to call foul, I commenced to wailing on it while it ran in a dizzy circle, trying to get out from under my fists.

On the third go-round, I noticed the other hornheads veering away from me and Jeff, and so I let go of my esteemed opponent and flung it back down the side of the hill. Just as the dinosaur broke the blue field, the scene changed and the honking para-sail-opolis landed smack dab in the middle of the Indian celebration.

# The Induction Window

Now, here's what I don't like about Indians. They have this strange, horse-like lizard land right in the middle of them, and what do they do? Do they start attacking the dinosaur? No, they look up at the hillside and start shooting arrows at us! Whoever called them savages wasn't far off. Ignoring a free meal, leather moccasins for the whole tribe, and who all knows what they could have made out of that weird-looking lizard, just to shoot at us. Talk about ungrateful.

So, Jeff and I hit the dirt again, and now we're both screaming at Nachenblitzen, and he's screaming back, and arrows are thudding into the ground all around us and some of them are embedding in Nachenblitzen's consoles and every time that happens, the field jumps like when you throw a rock into a pond. The next thing you know, the field up and surges and now Jeff and I are half in it, and half out of it. And wouldn't you know it, looming over us, looking for trouble, is Al O'Saurus.

I looked at Jeff and he looked at me, and we both leapt up at the same time, just as Al looked down and realized we were right underneath him. He was still coming up the slope of the hill and I had one good chance and so I took it. I handed him a haymaking clout on the underside of his jaw that broke my hand in three places, but the big lizard's head snapped back like it was on a spring hinge.

Then Jeff planted his feet and rammed all of his considerable bulk into Al's chest, lifting him up and away from the edge of the hill. That expression on Al's face was priceless as he tumbled back down the hill, ass over teakettle, and rolled to an upright position in the middle of the Mexican Banditos and the U.S. Calvary.

Al went nuts and pulled a guy off his horse and flung him into the stream with his jaws, and then he stepped on the horse and snapped it in two. The Calvary started shooting at Al, and then before I know it, here came all of the Mexicans up the trail from the creek bed, firing their guns right into the blue field and trying like hell to get away from the big lizard.

Jeff tackled me, knocking me sideways and away from the

hail of bullets and finishing the cracking job he done on my ribs earlier. As it was, I still got shot in the foot by one of the bandit's bullets, but Nachenblitzen's machine got the worst of it.

As the console sparked and sputtered, the blue window crackled and the disappeared like a soap bubble. The bandits and the Calvary and the dinosaurs and even those stupid Indians were gone. The machine wasn't through, though, and as Nachenblitzen jumped free of the truck bed, the consoles went up in a big, whooshing column of flame and smoke. That sorta started the truck on fire, and after that, we were too busy running for the now-empty creek bed to see what happened before the truck up and exploded.

I was dimly aware of a bright light that seemed to hang in midair for a minute, over us. Jeff later told me he thought that was the bald lightning that Nachenblitzen was looking for. I wish I had been conscious enough to appreciate it, but I was still dazed from the fall. That and getting shot in the foot, which hurt like a son-of-a-bitch. My hand wasn't a problem – I'd broken it before – but Al's jaw was without a doubt the hardest thing I'd ever punched, in or out of the ring.

With no truck and all of the equipment melted into scrap metal, we had to walk all the way back to Marfa in the darkness, thinking about what we'd all seen. I was suspended between Jeff and Nachenblitzen, who spent most of the trip crying like a little girl.

It turned out, the guy wasn't Nachenblitzen at all. He was a cardsharp by the name of Burbage, who won Nachenblitzen's rig in a protracted pinochle game. He heard enough about how the machine worked to try it out for himself, and thought he could sell the contraption to a foreign power. What they would want with a moving picture screen that shoots back at you, I'll never know. But he was pretty distraught about the whole thing.

Later, in El Paso, Jeff had a cane made for me, to help me get around, with one of the rocks from the mountain that he called quartz for a cane top. Every so often, if I hold it up in the right light, I can see old Al zip through the crystal.

And that's about it. Jeff saved my life, and I started taking it easy on him in our exhibition matches. We told a couple of people about that night, but no one believed us, not even Stumpy. So we stopped telling the story after a while. But we knew what happened.

Oh, yeah, we went back to the site the next day and walked around. Turns out, those Mexican bandits were bootleggers or smugglers or something, because we found their cache of hooch and brought it back onto the train with us, where we had a had a grand old time with it sharing with Ling Soo and his family – how I do dearly love a drunk Chinaman.

# SAILOR TOM SHARKEY AND THE REAL MCCOY

WORKING THE RACE tracks was fine. It was steady, and nobody minded me much there. In the off-season, I had a little leeway, I did some traveling up and down the coast of California. It was nice country. All man-made, you know, because you can't get water in a desert. But nice, all the same.

Well, in '32, I heard that Kid McCoy was getting out of San Quentin, so I thought it would be swell to have Jeff and Jack and some of the guys out to greet him. I made a few phone calls, but everyone I talked to was too busy and couldn't come out. In the end, I went by myself, which, now I think back on it, was probably not a good idea.

I drove down from Vallejo, where I'd been staying, and waited outside San Quentin for the big gates to open. Sure enough, here comes this short, sad sack-looking fellow in a straw boater and a blue suit. He's got a little valise with him, and even with my eyesight going, I could tell it was him.

"Hey, Charlie!" I yelled and waved.

McCoy looked up. When he saw it was me, he give out this wide grin – like we was at Madison Square Garden – and sure enough, there was Kid McCoy, like no time had passed since we last seen each other.

He come bounding over and shook my hand and clapped

my shoulder and I did the same to him. He thanked me for the surprise visit, and I didn't tell him it was because I felt bad I hadn't been to see him in the hoosegow. We piled into my Stutz and drove out of San Quentin toward Los Angeles.

Along the way, we stopped at a couple of diners and squared away some food, talking about the old days. I told him about my movie career, and he told me about his. Then we talked about my Vaudeville days, and he filled me in on what life was like in the hoosegow. Nobody bothered McCoy in San Quentin – despite his size, he was one of the best punchers in the boxing game, ever.

Back on the road, I noticed McCoy was getting down again. I asked him what the problem was, and he just broke down. Said his best years were behind him, that he was washed-up as a boxer, and oh, brother, the waterworks that came out of this guy! I didn't know what to do.

I waited until he sorta calmed down and then I said, "Gee whiz, Charlie, that's a rough deal."

McCoy sniffed and told me I was a good friend for putting up with his outburst. I didn't know about that. What I needed was a way to cheer him up. Sitting there next to McCoy, all I could think about was the good old days, when we were all boxing and McCoy was at the top of his game. Then it hit me.

"Charlie," I said, "I gots an idear. Let's go on a sightseeing tour!"

"What kind of tour?" McCoy asked.

"Well, for example, I know that island on the Rio Grande where Bob Fitzsimmons and Peter Mahar duked it out. You know, the fight Judge Roy Bean staged. We could go see that, for example. What do you think?"

I thought it was a pretty good idea. It beat watching the Mexicans pick oranges from the side of the road. It took a little more convincing on my part since McCoy thought I couldn't find my ass with both hands and a road map. I told him we weren't looking for my ass, we were looking for Texas. That settled the argument for him, and so we set off for the One Star State.

So, back we go to Texas. Now, I've got a lot of experience dealing with Texas, because I seem to have spent an awful lot of time there back when I was on the Vaudeville circuit. But here's what I have to say about Texas – every time I went back, something strange happened.

I don't mean strange like, "I lost my luggage," or anything like that. I mean strange, as in, "we got chased out of town by a bunch of seven foot tall half-wits throwing cactus plants at us." I know it sounds pretty weird, but that's Texas for you. Stranger'n crud.

Now, as we're driving to Texas, McCoy and I are making lists of other famous fight sites to go visiting. Turns out, there's a few of them in Texas, so this is good news. We figured we'd wing back up to New York eventually and I could re-introduce McCoy around to the guys. We take care of our own, and they'd all do right by him.

As to how we ended up in the town of Putatita del Fuego, on the Mexico side of the border in the Chee-hooa-hooa Desert, with three flat tires, I'll just say this in my defense. First off, the Rio Grande River is really damn long, and you can't just follow it to Judge Roy Bean's old town, because the roads don't go that way and I didn't know that. Also, McCoy kept yelling at me that he had to go to the bathroom and it was distracting my natural sense of direction. Then this big wind out of the North up and shoveled what must have been all of the sand in Montana in front of us, and I drove for about thirty minutes or so without being able to see the road or where I was going. So, anyway, that's how we ended up in Mexico.

I been to border towns before, like El Paso, which is pretty civilized, considering all of the Mexicans and Chinese people they got there that don't even fight or nothing, but this place wasn't anything like that. As I said, we blew out three tires when we run over an entire cow skeleton just lying in the middle of the road, like that's the best place to put a cow skeleton. We both got out of the car, cussing and kicking, but there's no use. I only had one spare for the Stutz, so we grabbed our luggage and made tracks for the town.

McCoy read the name of the town off to me, but neither one of us speaks Spanish, so we didn't waste time trying to figure out what it all meant. Besides, there was some kind of party going on in the streets and McCoy wanted to see what the hubbub was about, so we hoofed it over to the big crowd gathered in the middle of a cluster of sad-looking clapboard and adobe buildings. Not much of a town, if you ask me.

We sorta picked our way through the throng of people until we could see what was going on. I don't think neither one of us expected to see this short, slim, beautiful Mexican senorita, dressed in toreador pants, knee high boots, and a billowing white shirt. She had a sword in her hand she moved so fast that she would have given Basil Rathbone a run for his money.

She was faced off against a cowboy – and I mean, a cowboy, with the hat and the spurs, and the chaps, and everything. He was holding a sword, but it was pretty clear he didn't know what he was going to do with it. He was standing in front of two other cowboys, laid out on the ground with blood pooling up under them.

Behind the senorita was a young man, also Mexican, and dressed identically as her, and wearing a short cap besides. Sitting down behind them, on a big, carved wooden chair, was one of the most sinister looking Mexicans I ever seen. He was dressed in black, you know, like how those maharajah players dress, and he had leather bandoliers crisscrossing his body, and on his head was a sloping sombrero that kept his eyes in the shade and made him look like a vulture sitting on a roost.

The mean-looking Mexican grinned at the cowboy and said, "Well, Capitan? Ain't you gonna arrest us?"

Then the senorita winked at the cowboy, and he spat in the dirt and said, "Oh, the hell with this," and he dropped his sword and went for his gun.

I've never seen anyone quick draw a six shooter before except in the moving pictures, and let me tell you, this guy was fast, but as quick as he was, she was faster with the sword. He no sooner got the pistol out than she slashed him across the wrist and made him drop it. He howled bloody murder, dancing around and holding his wrist. Then the senorita stepped in again and before I knew it, she had cut out both of his eyes with the pointy end of her sword. The cowboy flopped, and the last thing his eyes saw was his own twitching body on the ground, right beside them.

The mean-looking Mexican and the boy with the sword cheered and clapped, and the crowd feebly joined in as they began to disperse. McCoy was pretty upset with the whole spectacle, so I dragged him out of there and spied the one word I knew in Spanish that would make everything better – cantina.

I got McCoy settled down at the bar and we ordered a couple of beers from the trembling fellow behind the counter. He must have recognized us or something, but was too shy to say anything. So, I called him back over and said, to help him break the ice, "Say, Friend..."

The bartender leaned in and whispered, "Listen, it is not safe here. I know why you have come."

"You do?" I said, surprised. "Well, then if you can just point us to the local garage, we'd be mighty grateful."

The bartender frowned. "Garage?"

"Yeah, and a tow-truck. My Stutz is marooned out there." I gestured back in the general vicinity of the road into town.

"Then you are not *Brujahs*?" he asked.

"Brew-ha-ha? What, like the fight outside? Naw, we don't want nothing to do with that. I'm just looking for some spare tires."

The bartender made a face at me like I was playing a joke on him, and then he looked over my shoulder and went chalk white. I heard the door to the cantina burst open and a voice yell out, "Tito! Tres Pollo Adobo, wey!"

I looked back, and sure enough, it was the mean Mexican and the two kids from outside. He locked eyes on me and I came to the immediate conclusion that we were going to have some trouble with this guy, and I don't mean maybe, neither.

He came sauntering into the cantina like he owned the place, his two kids behind him with their hands on their swords and their eyes on the crowd. No one inside the bar moved a muscle as the Mexican said, "So, look what comes slinking into town while everybody's back is turned – more gringos!"

I asked McCoy what the hell a green-go was, and he told me he thought it meant white man, so I resisted my urge to sock him for calling us names and merely turned away and took a long drink of my beer. But that wasn't going to do.

The Mexican came up and stood beside me at the bar. "What's your name, gringo?" he asked.

"I'm Sailor Tom Sharkey and this is Kid McCoy," I said.

"Baloney," said someone from the crowd.

"What?" I roared, wheeling around. "Who said that?"

A huge fellow, easily six feet tall and two hundred and fifty pounds, stood up and said, "He ain't Kid McCoy. He's too skinny and frail-looking. Him, Kid McCoy. Haw!"

I was about to intercept when McCoy put his hand up, a twinkle in his eyes. He turned around and said, "I don't want no trouble, mister," in a quiet kind of voice. "But I am Kid McCoy."

The man stood up and said, "Okay, then prove it. Let's have an exhibition match there, between you and that man-ape you got traveling with you."

Again, McCoy held me back with a gesture. He stared up at the guy, who was a full head taller and outweighed him by at least a hundred pounds and said, "Okay, we'll do that very thing." He walked over to the man and said, "But first, you need to tie your shoelaces."

The man looked down and said, "But I got boots on…" and that's when McCoy unleashed his famous corkscrew punch. I watched his fist almost spin all the way around as it found the underside of this guy's chin and it lifted him off of his feet and deposited him on his ass, picking imaginary daisies, in the corner of the room. It wasn't the hardest punch I'd seen McCoy throw, but it was enough to get the job done.

The cantina came to life, then, laughing and clapping in approval, including the big mean Mexican beside me. Someone threw the remnants of their beer on the out-cold fellow, and as he woke up, he shook his head and said, "Son-of-a-gun! That was the real McCoy!"

The mean Mexican beside me yelled, "Tito! Another round for the boxers!"

"Much obliged," I said. "Now, who might you be?"

"I'm surprised you don't know, Senor Sharkey." He stood back with a flourish. "I'm Miguel Barretos, and this is my town." He pointed to the boy and then the girl. "These are my children, Estaban and Carmelita." The twins gave me a leer and sat down at a large table in the corner of the cantina. "We would be honored if you would join us for lunch."

"Not at all," I said. "Always glad to meet a fan."

Well, everyone cleared a path for us, and we took our beers over and sat down opposite the three of them. A couple of helpers from the kitchen started laying out plates and forks and heaping bowls of rice and beans and this flatbread they call *tort-eelas*. We were hungry and so we started helping ourselves to the beans and rice.

While we were shoveling the food into our gobs, the three of them were watching us carefully, like we were going to pull a fast one. As I watched them watching us, I noticed Barretos' bandoliers didn't have any guns or bullets or anything like that in the pouches. I looked real hard and it seemed to me he had seven little wooden kewpie dolls, hand carved and hand painted, one stuffed in each pouch, and strapped to his front like a Indian woman with a lot of papooses. I sorta snickered at the thought, and I nudged McCoy, but he wouldn't look at me. He just kept eating his beans and rice, like I was going to get him in trouble, or something.

That's when Barretos swung his arm up and buried a Machete into the table. "What's so funny, Senor Sharkey?" he asked.

"Well, for starters," I said, "You've got a bunch of Kewpie dolls stuck to your chest."

Barretos' eyes lit up. "So, you know about the lucky magic dolls!"

"Yeah, of course I know about 'em," I said. "We used to win 'em by the handful at Coney Island."

"Aha, then you've come to try and win these dolls from me, is that it?"

I've met a number of puzzling characters in my life, but this guy was practically an imbecile. Shaking my head, I said, "Mister, all I'm after in this town is a new set of tires and a telephone."

Barretos was about to say something, but just then, the helpers from the kitchen brought out three whole chickens – and talk about strange! They were all upside down, on their backs, and they had knives sticking out of their breasts. They were covered in a red sauce that smelled great, but I never got a chance to try it because before I even knew what was happening, Estaban jumped up and grabbed one of the serving kids by the collar and slammed him into the wall. "You think that's funny, Wey?" he hissed.

Well, the kid was terrified and he started babbling in some foreign language – Mexican, probably, but I'm no language perfessor. The two of them were having a heated conversation, and then all of a sudden, Estaban drew his sword and drew it back like he was going to gut the kid.

I'd seen enough. I grabbed Estaban by the back of his collar and slung him away from the server. Estaban went sailing into a nearby table while the kid ran for the safety of the kitchen. When I turned back around, Barretos and Carmelita were standing, and McCoy was between me and them.

Estaban stood up and started yelling at me in that foreign tongue and I got mad and said that he should pick on someone his own size and then Barretos jumped in and said the chickens were a warning to his family and did I know what else, and I said no, what else, and then he jumped on the table and said he thought we were after his Kewpie dolls.

Kid and I started laughing at this, but these maniacs were serious. Before I knew what happened, Estaban lunged at me with his sword, an old cavalry saber from the looks of it. "Hold up," I yelled, scrambling out of the way. "This ain't a fair fight! Now, you just put down your sword and we'll settle this man-to-man…"

"No," said Barretos, "I think instead we will even the odds by giving *you* a sword!" He laughed and threw me the saber from where it was hanging at his waist.

I caught it with both hands and it wasn't a very suave maneuver, if you take my meaning. I don't know the first thing about sword fighting except what I've seen in the moving picture shows. So, I did the first thing I could remember Douglas Fairbanks doing and I jumped forward, swinging the sword high overhead in a kind of a circle.

That's when Estaban stabbed me in the shoulder.

I felt muscles seize up, like I'd been rabbit-punched there or something, and I almost dropped the sword in my hand. Estaban lunged at me again, and I did the first thing that came to mind – I slapped the blade away with my own.

It made pretty good sense, so I kept doing it. Every time Estaban made a lunge, I would smack the blade down or away. It got easier as I did it, but I realized I wasn't doing any attacking myself. Also, my arm was getting tired. He walked me backward around the cantina with everyone watching and shouting stuff at both of us.

This was ridiculous. What I wanted to do was drop the sword and punch his head inside out. Then it hit me – sword fighting was kinda like boxing. I just had to look for an opening. And since he was doing all of the attacking and none of the defending, I was betting he didn't have a lot on the ball. It was like going up against another slugger. I just had to wait for an opening.

Finally, I saw it. He would make two short lunges, and then a third, more powerful lunge. But every time he went for that third lunge, he'd drop his saber and cock his elbow straight out. So, the next time he tried it, I went smack, smack – beating his blade down – and before he could lunge again, I threw my saber out in a straight line and caught him on the sword arm with a deep gash.

The crowd cheered and Estaban came back at me with murder in his eyes. He started swinging free and generous, ignoring the fancy lunges he was doing earlier. All I could do was run backward and stay out of his way.

As I was running for my life, I dimly heard above the clamor, "Flop, Tom, flop!"

It was McCoy. He must have known something I didn't, so I literally pitched backward like I'd been cold-cocked and saw, for an instant, another sword pass through the space my chest had just been in. It was Carmelita, trying to stab me from behind. Instead, she caught Estaban in the throat, and Estaban's unchecked swing broke the side of her head open and they fell to the floor in a bloody mess.

I bounded back to my feet, and thanked McCoy for the warning. But he wasn't looking at me. Instead, the whole room had turned to face Barretos, his face a mask of rage and hate. "My ninos!" he cried, tears streaming down his face.

"Hey, lookee here, it was an accident," I said. "And anyway, that's what you get for teaching girls to fight with swords."

Barretos charged us both and knocked me down with his tackle. He began to rain blows about my head and face, screaming, "I'll kill you! You'll never get my magic dolls!"

The blows to the face weren't really bothering me all that much – I'd been hit much worse, and by experts. So I grabbed one of the dolls out of its pouch and said, "I don't want these stupid dolls! All I want is my car fixed, you numbskull!"

McCoy dragged Barretos off of me, which allowed me to stand up. I finally had enough room for a punch, with no distractions or swords, or any of that nonsense, so I made sure to put all of my beef behind it. I caught Barretos square on the chin, and that son-of-a-gun didn't move a muscle. He didn't even flinch, or blink, or nothing. He just gave me that stupid grin and said, "You can't hurt me, gringo! I am protected by the dolls!"

He gestured down at the bandolier and just as he did, it slipped off of his shoulder and then there was Kid McCoy, standing with the belt in his hand. "Catch, Tom!" he shouted, and threw it over Barretos' head.

The Mexican howled and made a desperate lunch for the belt, and we collided in mid-air. I took the opportunity to rabbit punch him a few times in the ribs as we fell to the floor in a mess of flailing limbs. A second later, I heard the crashing sound of breaking crockery. It was the lucky dolls. They had fallen out of the bandolier, and they were apparently pretty fragile, because they were all shattered into small pieces.

I almost apologized to Barretos, but when I looked over at him, he was shattered, too. I mean, literally. It was pretty horrible. But, I guess he wasn't kidding about needing them dolls to protect himself.

McCoy and I inspected one another for damage, and with the exception of my shoulder, pronounced ourselves fit to travel. We walked outside as a number of the townspeople ran into the bar and began working Barretos' remnants over like he was the last turkey leg at Thanksgiving. Apparently, he'd been bullying the town for some time.

We decided to at least go stash our bags back in the car and maybe try and push it into town. However, when we got there, we were shocked to find – and I'm not kidding here – all of the tires were restored to their previous condition.

If I'm lying, I'm dying. That town had the speediest mechanic I ever seen, proven by the fact he could change out my tires in an hour flat without hauling the car in.

I wanted to drive back into town to pay him, but McCoy talked me out of it, saying we helped the town get rid of Barretos, and now they would take the tire payment out of his hide.

So, we turned around and drove back up the Rio Grande. Eventually, we found the island where the great Fitzsimmons fight was fought, except it was mostly covered in water – so, pretty *auntie climactic*, on the whole.

Now, the funny thing is, ever since that road trip my Stutz hasn't broken down – not once. And get this…I haven't put gas in that car in three years, now. Not a dent, not a scratch, nothing. So, maybe there was something to them Kewpie dolls, after all.

# SAILOR TOM SHARKEY AND THE TINSELTOWN TERROR

BY THE TIME the circus train had pulled into Los Angeles, California, it was early December and I'd had enough of Larry Julius and his Cavalcade of All-Stars. And trains. And all of the other stuff that nearly got me killed on more than one occasion.

So, as soon as the cars stopped moving, I jumped onto the platform with my kit, shook Jim Jeffries' hand, give a wave to Stumpy the Goon – who was trying not to cry – and bid farewell to the Vaudeville Circuit.

I had this battered telegraph in my hand from a moving picture outfit calling itself Progressive Pictures. However, seeing as the telegram was pretty old, I thought I'd better call ahead first instead of just walking into a Hollywood studio and saying, "Here I am."

Also, I didn't know where the place was, or exactly who I was supposed to talk to, or anything else, for that matter. But I did know where sailors in town usually flopped, so I caught a taxi and was able to present my credentials and get a bunk in one of the hotels that catered to the sea trade.

Thankfully, there was a telephone at the front desk, so I called up Progressive Pictures and asked to speak to Jack Bachman. He got on the phone and I said to him, "This is Tom Sharkey."

"Who?" Bachman asked.

I had to remind him that he sent me a telegraph about six months ago, and he seemed kinda ticked off, and so I asked him didn't he get my reply telegraph and he said no, he didn't, and so that explained his bad attitude, I guess.

I managed to smooth things over with Bachman, and presently he agreed to send a car around to pick me up. As we drove through town, I couldn't help notice some of the streets weren't even paved, but the people walking along the sidewalks were coming out of really fancy and expensive-looking stores.

It reminded me of some of the boomtowns we'd played in, only a bit more civilized – you know, without all of the guns and people getting beat up outside of the stores and whatnot.

In the middle of the street, a group of fellows were planting a palm tree. It looked really out of place.

We drove a good ways down this one long street, out to the edge of town. Surrounding us were all of these big buildings looking like crop dusting garages, which was pretty much what they were.

Progressive Pictures was one of the buildings on this dirt road stuck out in the middle of nowhere. The driver explained to me each one of the buildings was a moving picture studio, which made me wonder how many movies were getting made, and if we needed that many in the first place. It wasn't as if they were going to replace a night at the theater or something like that. Of course, this was before the talkies, but I still think it's more of a gimmick than substantial entertainment.

I was let out and given some directions to these long, flat, bungalow-looking buildings. I walked up to the one painted pink with a big number 1 on the door and let myself in.

Inside was a small desk and one of the prettiest girls I'd ever seen sitting behind it. She was so pretty, she made my old ticker do a double take. I wanted to go to war for her.

She was on the phone, saying, "I don't have any control over her...well, no one does, except for her father, and he's..."

She saw me and covered the mouthpiece, and in a voice that

sounded like a sea lion with the scoots, barked out, "Deliveries go through the second gate!"

"Um, no, ma'am," I said, snatching my cap off of my head. "I'm here to see Jack Bachman. The name's Sailor Tom Sharkey." I stepped forward and closed the door. "And you must be the Queen of the Sweden, or something, only better, since I ain't never seen no squarehead doll that could hold a candle to you."

She just stared at me for a minute. I could see that she was chewing gum, on account of her mouth was hanging open. Maybe she was just a little slow, like Stumpy. So I said, slowly and distinctly, "I'm here for Jack Bachman."

She started, like something had goosed her. "Oh, gracious!" she shrieked. "Don't you hurt him! He's a good man! Whatever trouble he's in, he can work it out!"

I admit, that was just about the strangest greeting I'd ever gotten from a woman, and believe me, I've gotten some doozies. I've had women faint, bolt, get angry – one girl in Honolulu actually threw a serving tray at me and broke my nose – but this sure beat all.

"Aw, quit hollering," I said. "I've got an appointment. He's gonna put me in the moving picture show."

She clasped her hand over her bosom, which was a futile gesture, let me tell you, and then reached cautiously for the tipped over telephone like I might try to snatch it away from her. She banged on it a couple of times and then said, "Jack – 'er – Mister Bachman, some...person is here for you. He said he was a sailor and a loan shark."

"No, ma'am," I said, moving toward her, "I'm *Sailor* Tom *Sharkey*."

But even as I moved toward her, she backed cautiously away, keeping her desk between us, and screamed, "No, no...please hurry!"

I sighed. Perhaps it wasn't meant to be. Some dames are just too shy around a former celebrity such as myself.

She hung up the phone and said, "You just stay right there,

mister."

"Well, where else would I go? I just got here, lady."

Just then the door on the opposite wall flung open and a man entered, carrying a golf club and breathing heavily. Maybe he was being chased.

I stepped forward and stuck out my hand. "Hello, Mister Bachman. Tom Sharkey. Pleased to meet'cha."

Bachman was probably as old as me, but not nearly so broken in. He wore these little round glasses that he looked over, and his hair was plastered across his forehead just so, in a wave.

He lowered the golf club and ran his hand over his vest, smoothing it out. "Yes, hello, Mister Sharkey."

He shook my hand, which was a lot like grabbing ahold of a sweat rag. After that, he kinda stiffened up and said, "I was rather confused by your sudden phone call today. I had expected to hear from you much sooner. Six months ago, in fact."

"Yeah, but like I told you on the phone, I sent…"

"As it stands today, I'm afraid I don't have any time to give you a screen test, as we are in the middle of a production, and the shooting schedule is rather tight. Perhaps if you'd care to come back in January, we can make a proper appointment for then?" He folded his arms, like some kind of tough guy, and I realized he was doing it for the benefit of the secretary, who was watching us both like she was at a tennis match.

Well, I didn't feel like cooling my heels in Los Angeles for a month with no prospects. I also didn't like being the puppet in his he-man show for his secretary. So I did the only reasonable thing a man can do in these kinds of situations. I grabbed him by the lapels, jammed him backwards and pinned him against the wall, with his feet dangling a few inches off the floor.

With his attention focused squarely on me, I tried for a measure of diplomacy. "Trying to railroad me, hey? Well, Thomas J. Sharkey don't take no tests, and he don't stand around like a second rate citizen, neither. You either put me in the moving pictures here and now, or I'll grab you by the face and bowl your damn fool head down that dirt road outside!"

I then turned to the secretary, who had the phone in her hands and was holding it high overhead, and said, "Beggin' your pardon, Miss. You shouldn't have to listen to business negotiations such as this."

When Bachman started speaking again, it was in a much calmer tone of voice. "The, ah, force of your logic is well-stated, Mister Sharkey. If you could please put me down?"

I let him go, and the secretary handed Bachman his golf club. He took it from her with a doubtful expression. "Thank you," he said, straightening his tie. "Perhaps I was...a bit hasty in my assessment of your interest."

"That's more like it," I said.

"Yes, and now that I think about it, I think you would be absolutely perfect for the drama we are shooting right now." He smiled broadly, no doubt thinking about all of the money we'd make together. "Nancy, call over to Stage 'A' and tell Hogan I've got the perfect man for scene six."

"Well, that would be just swell," I said.

"Wouldn't it, just, though?" He turned to his secretary, who was smiling too, for the first time since I'd walked into the damn place. She was definitely a knockout, especially since I'd spent so much time in the company of Stumpy the Goon. After a while, you start thinking all imbeciles are dog-faced and you forget the world is a much bigger place.

Nancy picked up the phone. "Very good, sir. I'll tell them right away."

She picked up the phone and Bachman put his arm around my shoulders. "Come along, Tom, and I'll walk you down to the set." He took me back outside, into the sun, and steered me down a brick path leading around the side of the office and back to another hanger that looked a lot like a barn.

The doors were wide open to catch the breeze and people were running in and out of the building like they were rescuing stuff off a sinking ship, one armload at a time.

As we walked to the studio, Bachman explained to me the movie they were shooting was a modern day morality play, whatever that meant. "The part you'll be playing, Tom, is that of a convict in this prison."

"You mean, pretend, right? I'm not really going to jail?" I asked.

"That's right, Tom," he said. "It's called *acting*, and I think you're going to be great in the part."

"I'm no lubber, you know," I told him. "I been doing this for years, now, and I'm an old hand at it."

He cleared his throat, and started talking again in a slightly higher voice, "And you'll get to work with one of our rising stars. Her name is…"

But that was as far as he got, literally, because just then a coffee cup came sailing out of the open doors and shattered at our feet like a mortar shell. This was followed by a man yelling, "Holy Jehoshaphat!"

This man came running out in his shirt sleeves, one hand over his eye. He pulled up short when he saw Bachman and said, "I quit! I'll pick oranges with the Mexicans before I set foot on this lot again. Not while she's here."

I waited for Bachman to bawl the guy out and tell him to get back to work, but he merely nodded in a glum kind of way, like he wasn't surprised at all.

I was about to ask what was going on, but before I could, a woman's shriek echoed out of the studio. The man with the banged-up eye started, and then he hauled himself away in the other direction. I bounded forward, looking for the cause of such distress.

Inside, the studio was heat, darkness, and utter chaos. I could hear people moving around, shouting things, and a bunch of stuff happening, and I could see this white hot spotlight in the far end of the room, but everything else was roaring blackness.

Someone brushed up against me, and I hauled back a mauler to sock them, but it was only Bachman. "Come on," he snapped.

"Let's see what she's done now." And we started off toward the bright light.

That turned out to be where they were filming the movie. The lights were almost as bright as the ones they hung over Coney Island to film my fight with Jeffries. There weren't as many, though, and it lit up this one corner of the room that looked more or less like a hoosegow, only nowhere near as dirty, smelly, cluttered, and uncomfortable.

Once we got up close to the lights, we could see better, and most of the commotion was centered on a young girl, maybe twenty one or twenty two, who was in hysterics. But even if she wasn't in hysterics, she would have had every eyeball in the place glued to her.

She was short, and thin, but with a few curves. She looked a lot like pictures of the *little people*, you know, the fairies in the books? She had the big mop of red-brown hair and the most amazing eyes I ever looked into. Forget that blonde squarehead in the office, this girl was it!

"This," said Bachman with a heavy sigh, "is the star of our picture. Miss Clara Bow."

The little elfin woman heard her name and bounded over. "Oh, Jack!" she sobbed. "You've got to do something!" Her voice was a familiar Bronx nasal honk. She stopped crying when she saw me. "Say, I know you," she said. "You're Tom Sharkey!"

For the first time during our meeting, Bachman looked at me with a measure of respect. "Yeah, I am," I said. "Delighted to meet you, Miss Bow."

"Oh, gee, this is just swell," she said, beaming. "You were a legend in the old neighborhood where I grew up. Oh boy, if the guys could see me now." She lightly punched me in the chest. "My father's not gonna believe it. Tom Sharkey, in my movie!"

She grabbed my arm in hers, and then remembering she was upset, turned to Bachman and said, "They are all over me. I can't get any peace, any quiet. Then they tell me Daddy's doing it. I can't handle it, Jack. I need a cool down." And so saying, she dragged me off.

As we moved away from Bachman, she said, quietly, "I'm sorry about back there. Things aren't very professional around here right now. And I'm a mess. My father..." she trailed off and looked around. "I'm afraid we're going to have to find him. He's... probably outside, getting some air. You'll help me find him, won't you?"

"Well, sure," I said. "Anything for a fan, and a pretty one, at that."

"Thank you," she said, clutching my arm tighter, like she was afraid of something.

We didn't have far to look. Clara Bow's father was standing outside, slouched against the building and talking to himself. His eyes were sunken hollows and he looked like he hadn't eaten in a while. My first guess was, this guy was a rum-pot.

"Daddy?" she said, her voice suddenly very quiet. "Are you all right?"

The man blinked, stopped muttering to himself, and looked at us. "Clara!" he said. "She was here again!"

She let go of my arm and ran to her father. "No, Daddy, she's gone. She's dead. She can't be here."

He grabbed her roughly by the arms. "Oh, you'd like that, wouldn't you? Then you could do whatever you want, sleep with whomever you want..."

I could see Clara was crying again, so I stepped between them. "That's enough of that," I said. "I'm not one for getting into family mix-ups, but she's already upset, and you ain't helping."

"Daddy," Clara said quickly, "this is Tom Sharkey. From New York City. Remember?"

He blinked, and seemed to wake up again. "The fighter?" He shook his head, and it looked for a second like he would start crying, too. This was the weepiest family I ever had dealin's with.

"I used to listen to you on the radio all the time," he said. "You were my hero!" He grabbed my hand and shook it like it was a pump handle. "Mr. Sharkey, I want to tell you, that fight with Jeffries..."

I smiled politely, sure I was about to hear it all from round one. But some kid in a newsboy cap called them back in. "We're going in five," he said.

Clara and her father broke off and ran inside, and I followed at a more leisurely pace. I noticed as they walked into the studio, *Daddy* pocketed a worn silver flask. I knew it all along.

It was dark again when I walked inside, so I waited for my eyes to adjust before I started blundering around. Everyone was still running around, but this time, a bunch of folks were grouped around in front of the stage area.

Some woman was powdering Clara's nose, and now there was another man behind the bars of one of the jail cells. He had a lot of make-up on, too. I stood there and watched as everyone started shouting, and to please stop whatever they were doing, and on and on and on. Movie making is noisy work.

Eventually it got kinda quiet and then someone yelled, "Camera!" and this skinny man who was smoking a cigarette started cranking on the movie camera, and it made a pretty ferocious noise in the big warehouse.

A kid walked in front of the camera and yelled "Capital Punishment, Scene Five, take seventeen!"

Then the director up in front yelled, "Action!" and I watched as Clara ran up to the bars, crying hysterically, saying, "Darling, Darling."

The man in the cell tried to comfort her, but it was hard to do through the prison bars. They mumbled some endearments and then they pressed their faces up against the bars and looked up and out into the theater.

I turned around to see what they were both staring at, but I couldn't see anything special. The director yelled "Cut!" and everyone started clapping.

There was a short conference about what to do next, and then someone with a megaphone said, "Okay, let's get ready for Scene Six."

His bawling had an immediate effect on Clara, who suddenly came up off the stage – and I mean lifted vi'lently up off the ground about two feet. Her arms were outstretched like a bird, and she started blowing a torrent of obscenities at everyone, the likes of which I have never heard coming out of a woman's mouth—not even in Honolulu.

I'm no stranger to hard-boiled women-folk, but she was saying stuff that was so foul, I can't repeat it even now. Clara then turned on her father and called him everything but a white man. She ended her tirade with a scream of rage that rattled everyone's fillings and shattered the director's coffee cup, and then she ran sobbing out of the big metal barn.

Well, that was just not right. Remember, I've been around and I've seen a few things, so I know what I'm talking about. While everyone kinda stood around, figuring out what to do next, I took off after Clara. Her father had the same idea, because we slammed into one another, spilling out of the sound stage and into the hot California sun.

"Tom," he said, "maybe you can help her. She's...not herself. That's not my Clara."

"Well, gee whiz, what do you want me to do about it? I ain't got no luck with women and ponies – never could figure either of them out."

Her father hung his head and got a look on his face like he got caught swiping apples. "It's not like that, Tom. She's just very... sensitive. Her mother, you see..."

"Never mind," I told him. "Sensitive, eh? All right, let me go calm her down. Maybe I can get to the bottom of this scandalous behavior. Now, which way did she go?"

He looked grateful enough to cry. "She goes over to this other studio." He pointed down the street to another metal barn. "They're building a forest in there, and she likes it because it's quiet."

"Stay here," I told him. "In case she comes back."

He said he would, but I didn't believe him for a second. I ran into the other studio, which was just as dark as the one I'd just left. But I did see a soft glow of light. Creeping up on it, I could see Clara, a small candle at her feet, sitting in the middle of it all, on a stump. She was facing the fake trees, her back to me, and her body was shaking like she was crying. "Uh, hey there, kid," I said, as I strolled up to her. "How's about stowing the waterworks, and maybe..."

That was all I got out before she turned on me, and for just a second, I wasn't looking at that sweet, young Clara, but a much older woman. Then the illusion was gone and I was looking at Clara again. She snarled at me and gave me explicit directions for taking an immediate trip to the *infernal regions*, and while doing something to myself I never thought possible, either. Young or old, that kid had a mouth on her.

I waited for her to take a breath and then I stepped up onto the stage and said, "Now you need to watch that kind of language, young lady. Just because I used to be a sailor..." I was going to tell her about the time I traded insults with a Nepalese midwife for three days, but I never got that far. Clara jumped off of the fake stump and lunged at me, her eyes blazing bright red. She hit me square in the chest, like a medicine ball, only the force of her tackle blew me back off the stage, flat onto my back, with the wind knocked out of me.

"You can't have her back!" she screamed at me. "She's a whore! Unclean! She needs her medicine!" Her hands closed around my throat and right away my eyesight dimmed a few shades.

I didn't know what to do. She was sitting on my chest, heavy enough to keep me from catching my breath, and about to inflict some real damage on me. I had no choice, but to sock her in the puss, but that was against everything I stood for. I was about to throw a knee up and beg for forgiveness later when I noticed two things. Her father had come in, and was trying to get her attention, and the fake stage forest was on fire.

Clara's lunge probably kicked the candle over, but now we weren't a few yards away from a wall of flame. Clara's old man took out his flask, took a pull on it, and said, "Sarah! Get off him!"

"It's...Clara...not...Sarah..." I gurgled. Didn't this guy know his own daughter?

Clara looked up at her father, and I saw through my blackout haze that she had that older woman face again. "Harry?"

"Your daughter," he shouted over the roaring flames. "Look what you're doing to her!"

Clara looked down at me, horrified. Her face seemed to melt and shimmer, as if the heat was getting to her. It was sure getting to me. I watched as a dark, fast shape flew out of Clara's open mouth, heading for her father. He panicked and threw up his hands, including the one with the flask still in it. There was a flash of bright light, and then the flask was glowing red—just like Clara's eyes were a few minutes ago. Clara slumped off of me, unconscious, and I managed to stand up without too much trouble. She was considerably lighter now.

Her dad looked horrified, like I'd done something wrong. Maybe he was just realizing the seriousness of our predicament. He shook the flask and quickly screwed the cap on. "Tom, come on!" he said.

I scooped Clara up and we ran for the exit, choking and gasping. The fire brigade was in full force when we caromed out of the building, and they were busy throwing water on the neighboring buildings, the three of us, and everything except where the fire actually was.

They later told me this was to contain the fire. I thought the idea was to put the fire out, but then again, I ain't no fireman. They had a doctor look us over. Once we were pronounced all right, Jack Bachman ran up and started bawling us out. Ordinarily, I wouldn't have took it from that guy, but we did sorta burn down his studio.

Clara didn't remember what happened. When I asked her who Sarah was, she got quiet and confessed that it was her mother. Her dead mother.

Harry said something about a *dybbuk*, whatever the hell that was, and he explained ever since her mother died, the woman had been haunting the two of them.

He also told me a bunch of private things, like how screwy in the head his dead wife had been, how she almost killed Clara one night with a butcher knife, and a bunch of other things that are kinda private and embarrassing, so forgive me if I don't relate them to you.

Just know Clara's mom was a real nut job who wouldn't let a little thing like death keep her from trying to insert herself into Clara's life.

All of that personal family talk made my head swim, and I was treading my own water when Jack Bachman came back up to me and thanked me for burning the building down.

It seemed there was some film they were planning, and it was going to cost them a steamer trunk of money to make it. However, since we accidently set fire to the set, the insurance company would have to pay them and they could cut their losses. I didn't really care one way or the other. I just wanted to be in the movie I was supposed to be in.

They eventually shot my scene. I played a convict who made trouble for Clara's love interest. It wasn't too hard, especially since I didn't have to speak out loud where people could hear me. I got paid for my day's work, plus some of the insurance money to keep my mouth shut, and that was more than enough to drop anchor in L.A. and pursue my new career in the movies.

Clara, of course, went on to be a big famous movie star, but I heard tell of some of her exploits along the way, and it made me think maybe she hadn't shook off the ghost of her mother, after all.

# SAILOR TOM SHARKEY AND THE ELECTRIC GORILLA

NINETEEN SIXTEEN WAS a hell of a year for me. First, I lost my horse stables in Frisco, due to owing a number of gambling debts. Then, Florence left me when she figured out I wasn't swimming in dough no more and she wasn't going to ever be any kind of actress. She took off to Reno, and I didn't see her until the divorce trial a month later.

Somebody told me she ended up working as a spiritual medium or something along those lines. I don't know much about that, but in the Vaudeville circuit, all of the women in the spirit medium racket were really just flexible con artists with the ability to hide large noisemakers in their womanly places. It sounded like something Flo would have been pretty good at, come to think of it. I never was any good at picking dames.

Well, I was stewing in my own juices when I got a telegram from a guy who was putting on an exhibition of the scientific demonstration of pugilism and wanted me to be a part of it.

I cabled him back sayin' there wasn't nothing scientific about my pugilism, and then he cabled me back sayin' he knew that, but wanted my strength and staying power in the ring. So, I cabled him back to ask how much the job paid, and he cabled me back sayin' if I went on the lecture circuit with him I could make at least five grand.

Now, that wouldn't put a dent in what I owed people. But it was a start. So I cabled him back and said okay if he coughed up the dough for travel. His answer was to cable me back train tickets to New Orleans.

The last time I was in New Orleans was years ago when I was in the Navy. My memories of New Orleans were all mixed-up with my Navy days – watching John Sullivan lose to Jim Corbett, and stuff like that.

I'd heard about the big hurricane that hit New Orleans the year before, and I was a little excited to see the place now they had rebuilt it. So I threw my gloves and trunks into my grip and bid a fond farewell to San Francisco – the city what hit me below the belt.

The train ride wasn't nothing to write home about. It was long, but it was first-class, so that helped.

A few people recognized me and I signed some autographs for folks and they asked me about the big Jim Jeffries fight, and I told 'em what they wanted to hear – I gave 'em a run-down of the damage Jeff done on my carcass.

Everyone always wants to know how I could have taken all that punishment – the three broken ribs and all of that – and still been on my feet after twenty five rounds. I always tell 'em I just didn't have enough sense to sit down.

I got excited when the train pulled into New Orleans. It looked exactly the same as when I'd visited there over ten years ago, only it looked completely different, too.

There was a lot of new buildings and a new bridge and more boats and a lot more people all working on the docks, loading paddle boats and trucks and train cars. It reminded me of the Navy.

I no sooner stepped off the Pullman when I was surrounded by a small clutch of duded-up looking swells, all top hats and tails. They was acting like I was still in the fight game, the way they clapped and cheered for me.

I was too dumbfounded to do anything other than smile and

nod. Eventually, all of the men had shook my hand and the last one introduced himself as Dr. Templeton Cain. I told him I was Tom Sharkey, and they all laughed.

"So, what's with all of this fanfare and hooey?" I asked Cain.

He beamed down at me, and I noted he and the rest of the men were all considerably taller than me.

"Mister Sharkey, these men are members of the Galton Foundation — our benefactors in the lecture circuit we are about to undertake."

"Undertake?" I said. "As in funeral arrangements?"

This drew another round of laughter, but I didn't join in. I was serious. What kind of a lecture tour had I signed up for?

Cain ignored my question and continued, "Tonight, we will enjoy a sumptuous repast, and I will deliver the first part of my lecture on the advancement of human thought. Tomorrow, we will convene on the docks for the second part of the lecture for a physical demonstration of the principles I will expound."

Well, I took all of that in, but it really didn't make a lick of sense to me, so I patted him on the shoulder and said, "You just tell me who you want me to spar with, Doc, and I'll do the rest. I've done so many of these things, I coulda sleepwalk through 'em."

Cain chuckled. "Come," he said, taking my luggage from me and leading me back into the group of swells. "We'll go to the hotel and freshen up before the lecture."

The thought of a hotel with food and a shower stomped all over the other questions I had for Cain, so I let him lead me to a taxi. I was starting to feel like a heavyweight again, and it got me awfully curious about what the Foundation actually foundated, so I asked Cain and he rattled off a bunch of names like Eugene Nicks and things like *Friendology*. I didn't know anyone named Gene Nicks, but Friendology sounded okay in my book and I told him so. Cain spent the rest of the cab ride back to the hotel staring at my head and muttering to himself.

These Galton Foundation yeggs weren't kidding. We pulled

up in front of a hotel that looked like the governor's mansion. I gave Cain a look and he waved it off.

"They're taking care of everything, Mister Sharkey. All you have to do is what you do best."

I guessed he meant take a punch.

We walked inside the lobby and got attacked by porters and other folks in red monkey suits, ushering us one way while my luggage went the other.

This was better than the joints in New York, and that's saying something. I was whisked to the elevators and fairly dumped into my room only to find my luggage had beat me there. That's service, by heck!

Cain started to rattle off more instructions for me, but I was exhausted from all of the travel. "Listen, Doc," I told him. "All I need to know is when and where the lecture is tonight."

"Seven o'clock," he answered. "In the main ballroom. But, Mister Sharkey, I want to make sure you understand..."

"Belay that," I said, as gentle as I could. "All I need is a little shut-eye before the big *to-do*. Don't worry about me, Doc. I'll be dressed and ready to impress at seven, sharp."

"Oh, well, that's a relief," he said.

I left him to his muttering and went upstairs to flop for a couple of hours. When I woke up, I had a little appetite, so I ordered up some room service and polished off a chicken and some potatoes.

After that, I took a quick shower and was feeling right as rain. So, I changed into my fighting togs, donned the special robe I used for exhibition matches with my motto, *Don't Give Up The Ship*, across the back, and hung my gloves over my neck.

I looked at myself in the mirror; not bad for an old dub. I took the stairs in order to warm up a little, and as I sprinted into the main lobby, I spied the double doors at the other end. The ballroom! I lowered my head and made for it at a steady gallop, stiff-armed the doors, and made my gallant entrance.

I was in the main ballroom, all right. It was almost as big

as Madison Square Garden, but there wasn't no ring set up, I noticed. Nor was there any roped off area. In fact, all I could see was shocked, pale faces and stiff suits. The place was filled with high society types, all piled up hair and formal dresses, all making their way to long banquet tables. Everyone had been talking, but at my entrance, the whole room fell silent and they were all staring at me like I was a whore in church.

Finally, I spied Cain running over to me. He was in a monkey suit, too, and I got the distinct impression I was maybe a little underdressed for this whole affair. "What's the matter with you?" he hissed. "You said you'd be dressed!"

"I am dressed – for fighting!" I protested. "I thought we were demonstrating tonight."

Cain made a growl in his throat, and whispered, "If anyone asks, tell them this was part of our publicity campaign."

He turned away from me, all smiles, and said to the room, "Ladies and gentlemen, may I present Tom Sharkey, one of the most colorful and storied fighters in boxing, as our special guest to help with our lecture circuit!"

There was a smattering of applause, and then everyone started talking some, but I could tell whatever they were talking about before, they were discussing me now.

Cain steered me away from the door and we proceeded to make the rounds on the way to the table up to the front of the room. Everyone had a Dutch name like Van Der Swiller or Von Frachus, and let me tell you, I'm not entirely certain about this, but there seemed to be an unusually high number of *squareheads* in attendance.

This was not a real accurate repersentation of the New Orleans populace. The only black people I saw were all wearing waiters' get-ups. Everyone else looked like well-dressed pitchers of milk.

One of the pitcher-women regarded me through her glasses on a stick and make a snorting noise. "Really, Dr. Cain," she said, "I don't care for the so-called sport of boxing. I find the activity to be brutal in the extreme. Are you sure employing this...*pugilist* is strictly necessary for the cause?"

Cain started to say something, but I beat him to it. "Madame, I didn't catch your name, but I see you have your son with you." I motioned to the rotund-looking squarehead boy trailing in her wake. "Mighty fine looking boy, madam, but I wouldn't own him if he were a coward, nor would you. And furthermore, I think every boy oughtta be taught how to fight."

Seeing the expression of horror on her face, I quickly added, "I don't mean he should go looking for it. But he ought to know how, in case anyone should insult his mother." The woman made a weird sound, and Cain quickly marched us away from them.

"I think that went well," I said, pleased I'd got my point across and defended my chosen profession at the same time.

Cain gave me an odd look and said, "Why don't you sit down at our table, here? I'll be back in a minute."

People were taking their seats and I noticed most of the welcoming committee from the train station was arranged at my table. The waiters came out and served us food in courses, which I never could understand. I prefer my chow on one plate, where I can see it all at the same time. One plate at a time feels too sneaky for me, and I've had more than one of these fancy dinners blow up in my face because I didn't like the looks of what came after the spinach salad.

This meal was okay, though, but I passed on the turtle soup. You only have to be shipwrecked off the coast of Pago Pago for three weeks once in your life to never want to eat a turtle again.

I told my dinner companions that story, but they didn't seem to appreciate it very much, until Dr. Cain spoke up and said, "You see, gentlemen? Ingenuity, adaptability, and resilience. Admirable traits, all, I would say."

They nodded in agreement and he went on. "Not to mention, Mister Sharkey's legendary stamina and endurance in the sport of boxing."

One of the top hats asked me, "We're very pleased to have you in this capacity, Mister Sharkey. How much do you know about our foundation?"

"Oh, I'm all caught up, thanks to Dr. Cain, here."

"Really?" he said. "Then you're familiar with Goddard's work with the Kallikaks?"

"Goddard?" My eyebrows shot up. "Kallikaks? I don't know who they are, but I actually saw *Joe* Goddard knock Choynski through the ropes whilst I was on shore leave in Australia."

They all looked confused by my recollection. I don't know why. I wouldn't lie about a thing like that. Another one of the top hats said, "Tell me, Mister Sharkey, how far back does your family go?"

"Go back? Buddy, they never left."

Cain laughed and I said, "They're in Dundalk, Ireland, and they couldn't be prouder of their son."

With that, two or three of the swells excused themselves from the table. Everyone else looked down at their strawberries and cream.

Cain leaned over and said, real quiet, "I must apologize for some of my colleagues. The Irish question is far from settled within the foundation. You understand, I trust. Myself, I count no white men amongst my enemies. All the same, it would be best if we left your ancestry off the table during this lecture tour."

I nodded and sat there a while, looking at them all and thinking to myself. In all of my years of traveling, my Irish accent got kinda lost in the shuffle, but I remember what it was like when I first came to America.

The Jewish kids used to throw rocks at us every day after work, and they called us names. Pretty mean stuff, if you want to know the truth, but it toughened me up considerable. Still, I was young and didn't have anyone to stand in for me. That's how come I originally went to sea for a few hitches with the Merchant Marine, and later the U.S. Navy. I figured if I was going to get called a bunch of names I didn't understand, I wanted it to be by weird-looking people in foreign countries.

I got so lost in my reverie, I missed Cain's introduction.

Everyone stood up and clapped for him as he sorted his notes out on the podium. He spoke in a clear, loud voice that filled the room. To make matters worse, he talked for over an hour. Oh, boy, was this stuff over my head!

He blew a lot of hot air about breeding, good stock, families, and something about producing a race for superior intelligence. I didn't exactly know how you'd conduct a race for intelligence. Maybe you'd time people doing math problems, and the first one to solve them all would win the trophy or the ribbon. Pretty boring, if you ask me, but what did I know. If this was the Foundation's racket, I figured they had an uphill go of it.

At the end of the lecture, Cain explained his developmental breakthrough would be unveiled tomorrow at the docks, after which me and him would journey up the Mississippi by paddleboat, ultimately making our way into New York, giving lectures and demonstrations. That got him a round of ear-splitting applause.

I still didn't know what the hell he wanted me for. I've never felt so out of place in my life. As soon as the applause died down, I beat feet for the bar and spent the rest of the night surrounded by fans, talking about Bob Fitzsimmons and Jim Corbett.

Cain came around the next morning and we had breakfast together. Over a couple of poached eggs and toast, I said, "So, is this the day I finally get to hit something?"

Cain nodded through a mouthful of coffee. "Yes," he gasped. "It's very simple. I'll have a special instrument in the arena designed to test your reflexes, your strength, your endurance and your agility."

"But, you want me to box, right?"

"Oh yes. You'll attack, defend, and feint as normal." Cain chuckled. "I'm counting on you to do your best and put the machine through its paces."

"Okay, then," I said. "I'm going to punch stuff. That's all I wanted to know."

"Just relax," Cain said. "I'll walk you through the routine the first few times. The crowd will appreciate it. After a while, you'll be able to handle the demonstration on your own."

I told him I wasn't very good at memorizing things and he told me there wasn't anything to memorize and, in fact, it'd be better if I didn't try, but just acted on instinct.

That suited me, since I never put much thought into my fighting. We parted, with instructions on where to meet him later at the docks, and I spent a few pleasant hours walking around, taking in the town and eating those goofy doughnuts without any holes.

By the time I made my way to the docks, a sizeable crowd had gathered. It was mostly the swells from last night, but there were a number of the general citizenry standing around and gawking at the tall dock that had been converted into a speaking platform.

On the far side, by the stairs, was a podium and a microphone. In the middle of the platform was a curtain held in place by a makeshift boom. The curtain was suspended on four sides, to hide what was sitting up there.

Cain had brought all of my luggage down to the docks, so we could leave right after the exhibition, so I changed into my fighting togs behind the platform.

"Are you ready?" Cain asked, looking me over. "Let's get started."

"Where do you want me?"

Cain blinked. "Why onstage with me, of course."

"Yeah, but what do you want me to do."

"Look, it's very simple. Just stand there until I introduce you to the crowd, and then we'll begin. Follow my lead, all right?"

"You're the doc," I said, climbing up the stairs behind him. As soon as Cain was visible to the masses, a great cheer broke out. I got up there and looked out over the crowd. Wasn't nothing I'd never seen before, but it felt more like the day before an election rather than a scientific demonstration of pugilism.

Cain started to talk, and again, I had trouble following him. More of this *intelligence race* nonsense, and how diluting blood lines made for a nation of imbeciles. I'm approximating what he said, but it was stuff along those lines. Then he motioned over to the curtain.

It came up all at once, and the crowd gave a gasp like they are supposed to do, and I was looking at a six foot tall electric gorilla. At least, that's what it looked like to me.

"Behold," Cain said, stepping away from the podium. "This mechanical marvel you see before you was once a steam engine. In fact, it was the very steam engine John Henry, the Negro steel-driving man, defeated in the legendary contest before he succumbed to exhaustion. On that day, it was said, that the Negro bested the machine. But what do you think happened to this machine after John Henry was laid to rest? Nothing! It lay there, broken, but eminently repairable, for almost four decades."

I had heard the story of John Henry, but this thing standing in front of me didn't look nothing like a steam engine. It was all cylinders, big gears, and cast iron metal. It had pistons and solid steel beams for arms, and twin red glowing eyes that got brighter and brighter as Cain spoke.

"When I discovered this machine, I recognized there was value in its various components, but more important – rebuilding the machine into the humanoid form you see before you serves to demonstrate that it took a superior intellect to craft and create such a thing. What was, to the common Negro, little more than a scrap pile, has been transformed into a sophisticated device for use in the military and the police force in the suppression of riots. The suppression of riots! This *mere machine* will actually save lives!"

Everyone started cheering and clapping. Make that, everyone in the Foundation. The general populace of New Orleans didn't look too thrilled at the prospect of dealing with an electric gorilla, and neither was I.

The arms on the thing were on a swivel joint and they were almost as long as its whole body. At the end of each arm were two clamps that locked and made an O-ring of solid steel.

Dr. Cain basked in the cheering for a minute and then

waved them down. "In order to demonstrate the effectiveness of the mechanical marvel, former heavyweight great, Sailor Tom Sharkey, has graciously agreed to put the machine through its paces. Are you ready, Tom?"

I looked over at him and addressed the crowd. "As ready as I'll ever be."

The machine buzzed and suddenly rattled to life. It came out of a crouch and was suddenly about six feet tall, and its legs were actually a platform with wheels on four sides. I thought it was the palette they rolled it in on at first, but then I saw it was all of a part. The eyes were white hot now, and I could feel electrical current coming off of the thing.

"It's gonna shock me, Doc!" I said.

"What you're feeling, Tom, is the electrical field used to sense incoming attacks and deflect them. The current is harmless, save for a slight tickle."

Cain walked over and slowly raised his hand from his waist and said, "Greetings," and the robot lifted its claw and shook hands with the doctor. The crowd went nuts, and even the general citizenry looked impressed.

"Simple movements, gentle movements and so forth, interrupt the current at a certain speed," Cain explained, "and the machine replies accordingly. But if I set the machine to a defensive stance..." He reached into his pocket and did something and, suddenly, both arms folded and tucked in and the claws rotated into O's and, aside from the fact it didn't have no legs, the electric gorilla looked ready to fight.

I looked over at Cain. He said, "Go ahead, Tom, give it your best Sunday punch. Let's see if you can get through Humano's defenses."

I looked at the machine. It didn't have no expression. No sweat on its brow. No eyes to try and read. Nothing to give it away for me. I might as well have been boxing a Packard. I took a deep breath, waded in, and swung a high, fast right, aiming for the square-grilled jaw.

Quicker than I could see, the machine's torso spun and its right arm shot out and the claw smacked against my wrist and clamped down on it. The torso kept rotating, pulling me with it, and when it completed its spin, the claw let go and threw me down in front of the podium. Everyone clapped and cheered as I got up and dusted myself off.

"Well, I sure wasn't expecting that," I said to Cain, who beamed at me. "May I try again?"

"Certainly, Tom. You may *have at it*, as they say."

Okay, so this big metal bastard wasn't fighting by the Marquis of Queensbury rules. That was good. I could actually scrap without worrying about a referee calling foul on me. I decided to dispense with the technicalities and wade in with both fists flying.

I stalked forward, swinging wide and generous, and I heard Cain dimly say, "You see, Ladies and Gentlemen, whenever Sailor Tom enters the low-voltage electrical field, sensors on the robot react in accordance to where the field has been broken. This simulates the eyesight in a normal human, of course..."

While he was yammering on, I had thrown a variety of my best rights and lefts, the likes of which would have taken anyone else's head off, had they landed. However, those big, pin-wheeling arms kept rotating and knocking my fists out of the air even as I was counterpunching. I felt like a flat-footed dub fighting this scrap metal monkey, and it was irritating me more than somewhat.

I backed off, my arms numb to the elbow from hitting the I-beams this thing had for wrists. No sooner did I put my guard back up when that monster's long, slicing left actually looped around my gloves and caught me in the side of the head.

I dropped to the ground with a bunch of Chinese gongs going off in my ears. What a punch! It felt just like getting hit by a horseshoe thrown by an elephant. I got up quickly, but the robot had backed off.

The crowd was laughing and clapping like they'd just seen a show. Cain was talking again, but I couldn't hear him for the ringing in my ears and the roaring fighting Irish blood surging through me. I wasn't going to be made a fool of, not by some scrap metal monkey.

I charged the thing with a roar of rage and made for the robot's bread basket. Or where his stomach would have been, had it been a man. My left crashed into the metal. Had I not been wearing gloves, the impact would have reduced my knuckles to Chiclets.

I followed with a right and while the robot was dealing with my hands, I head butted him right in his jaw. That made the ringing in my ears stop, but it started the blood flowing as the sharp metal edge of its jaw opened a gash over one eye.

I rocked back, but I guess I was still in the electrical field or something because both robot claws started spinning in my direction. I blocked the first few blows, but as my arms went numb under the relentless hammering, my guard slipped and both sets of claws rained down on my head, neck and shoulders again and again.

I felt my knees give out and the floor came rushing up to greet me. I hit the ground hard and I no sooner tried to get up, but here he came again, pressing the advantage.

He was all over me. I covered up, feeling weak and helpless, and those hammering claws kept whaling on my back. He was beating me down, and as I fell to my knees, I appreciated the savagery of the attack. Merciless. Uncompromising.

"You see?" boomed Cain. "Again Mister Sharkey goes down. Every time he gets up, Humano will be there to keep him contained. Any threat will be assessed and dealt with. Let me state this next point, very emphatically – this kind of precision instrument could only have come from the Aryan mind. A mind bred true and pure, through undiluted bloodlines. This device couldn't come from the mind of the Negro. As a race, they are not creators, but destroyers!"

I heard all of this, dimly, through the cheers of the crowd, and I scanned the sea of people for a face I recognized. What I found were a whole lot of worried-looking black folks.

Their clothes were shabby, and they were working the docks, or they were doing some other kind of day labor. But they all were watching me, and I realized something. Me and them had a lot more in common with each other than I did with this Cain fellow.

I knew honest work. I'd starved before. And I knew what it felt like to be a man, and be called an animal. Irish, black, Chinaman, it didn't matter none. People were people. I learned that in my travels.

Different ain't better any more than it's worse. And furthermore, all of that Aryan superiority talk was a bunch of horse-pucky. I'd boxed Jack Johnson before in sparring sessions and there was no disputing who the best boxer of any skin color was.

I got up, and Cain said, "Even with his vaunted endurance, Mr. Sharkey surely must admit this mechanical marvel is an effective and skillful tool for crowd control and management."

I said, "It would certainly appear that way," and I held out my hands. "Would you be so kind as to unlace my gloves?"

"Of course," said Cain, smooth as you please. "Let's all give Tom Sharkey a round of applause for his courageous demonstration," he said to the crowd. They clapped while Cain fumbled with my laces. As soon as my gloves were loose, I dropped them at his feet and charged the machine, bare-handed.

It took the crowd a few seconds to figure out what was going on, and by then, I had the electric gorilla in a clinch. Those elbow joints were great at keeping people at bay and delivering snapping punches, but in close like this, the claws got more in the way of one another as they tried to hammer on my exposed back. I didn't care none.

With my fingertips, I was trying to do something I couldn't do with the gloves on. I was looking for a seam or a joint that I could work on. Finding nothing on the drum-barrel body, and there being no refs on hand to call foul, I went for the face and the eyes with my bare hands.

The robot starting making a whistling sound, high-pitched –

like a little girl's scream. That's when the torso started spinning freely around with such force I found myself having to hang on for dear life.

I managed to get my fingers under the thing's huge chin and climbed on its back like a wrestler. This put me in reach of those strong arms again, but before they could catch hold of me, I gripped the thing's head in both hands and ripped the topmost part of its face clean off. There was an assortment of gears and belts and other things in the head and neck, and I reached in and grabbed a handful of whatever was handy and ripped it out in pieces and chunks.

Those arms caught me by the shoulders. Had I not curled my legs around the stump of the robot's neck, they would have dashed me to the boards, head first.

I used my whole body to pull us down, and both me and the robot toppled over onto our asses. The robot's arms let go and tried to tip its body back over, but with the robot on the ground, it was easy to wade into the body with both hands and start the dismantling process in earnest. I grabbed the right arm at the ball joint and wrenched it off like pulling a chicken leg out of the socket. This I tossed to the crowd, along with an assortment of spare metal parts and a sprinkling of language that need not be repeated here.

I removed the other arm the same way and used it to beat open the chest cavity, cracking it open like an oyster pried wide, and I threw the bits and pieces over my shoulder. My hands were all cut up from the gears and steam pipes inside, but I didn't care – and from the howls of approval from the audience, neither did they.

Amidst the carnage, a number of men pulled me off of the scattered remnants of the robot. It looked more like a steam engine now, and less like some Aryan brain race winner thing. Steam and oil and sparks were emitting from the scuttled carcass, and I kicked some of the stray pieces and parts in the intentional direction of the squareheads on the committee and told them to go piss up a rope.

That's when the crowd surged onto the stage and lifted me up on their shoulders, to the dismay of Dr. Cain and the rest of his squarehead friends.

Most of the colored folks, and a fair number of the Irish folks, too, slapped me on the back and congratulated me on my technical knockout. I retrieved my grip, looked over my shoulder at the group of swells standing over the shattered remains of their riot control robot, and blew them a fat raspberry. Then me and two hundred of my new friends crowded into the nearest bar we could get to and drank ourselves silly.

Needless to say, I didn't get paid for the appearance. Not one of those duded up swells offered to pay for my ticket back to Frisco. However, when I explained my situation to my friends at the bar, they passed the hat around and put in enough dough to cover my trip home.

One of squareheads threatened me with legal action, but when I showed him the scars on my hands from fighting their electric gorilla, he turned even paler than before and beat a hasty retreat. What's funny is, as I was waiting at the train station, I heard someone shout my name, and who do you think it was?

"I'm glad I caught you," Dr. Cain said, running up to me all out of breath. "Listen, we can still salvage the lecture circuit."

"How's that?" I said. "Your big robot is scrap metal. And how come you ain't mad at me?"

"Oh, I was, to be sure," he said, and then lowered his voice. "Look, I'm an inventor, see? I go where the funding takes me. Here, what we'll do is rebuild the robot, but not as a robot. It'll be a man in a suit, and we'll pit the machine age against homespun American religious values."

"I don't know," I said, rubbing my chin. "Do I really want to fight that thing five times a week, just to sell some bibles – or whatever your racket is this week."

"No, Mister Sharkey, you misunderstand me. You would actually be inside the robot suit."

I'd like to set the record straight about my second divorce here and now. The press said it was a bitter one, and said I was holding out because I loved Flo, but that's just not the case.

I wasn't hiding out in New Orleans for a month because I didn't want to be served with the papers. No, I'd taken as big a swing at Cain as I could manage and not only was it big enough to plow into him, but also took in a tin star who was passing by at the time.

I got thirty days in the jug for slugging the cop – with five days' *time served* for knocking out the inventor.

# SAILOR TOM SHARKEY AND THE PHANTOM OF THE GENTLEMAN FARMER'S COMMUNE

It wasn't all fun and games traveling with Lawrence Julius Cavalcade of Super Stars Vaudeville show. Sometimes, it could get downright scary. I almost didn't live through my first two weeks. After I solved the mystery of the phantom of the Gentleman Farmer's Commune, things settled down more than somewhat, and shortly after that, Jim Jeffries joined the tour, and then I had someone to pal around with.

My first real friend on the circuit was Stumpy the Goon. He sorta looked up to me, I guess, which is natural, considering my status. He used to be with the Halloran Brothers Circus, but their outfit went broke when their fat man, Colonel Rotundo, suffered a fatal heart attack and fell on top of Ten-Gallon Alan, the world's tallest midget and killed him, thus ending the careers of their two best draws.

They called Stumpy Bingo the Dog-Boy on account of his distinctly canine features, and some of the extra body hair, and the fact he was an imbecile in that kinda always happy way, like a dog.

Anyway, he was their official geek. This struck me as silly, since I never saw Stumpy make a ferocious face in his life. On the other hand, he did like the chickens which I'm told is pretty essential in the geek trade. This is where the trouble started, I figure.

I came on the show, joining for a one week engagement in Chicago, along with a couple of other acts, including the Ling family of acrobats – a group of what seemed like thirty-seven Chinamen of all different shapes and sizes – and a dapper looking gentleman named Colonel Strathmore and his mummy box.

The Colonel sold patent medicines to the rubes, and if you paid him a dime, he would show off some withered looking remnants in a lacquered wooden box and recount the tale of the infamous Liver Eatin' Johnson.

This liver eatin' guy was pretty horrible from what I could tell, but Colonel Strathmore knew the story so well he could really make it come to life. He was the only guy I ever met who could class up a story about a cowboy cannibal and make you care about the Indians he was killing and eating.

Anyway, we all came on in Chicago and Stumpy was the guy who helped me with my bags. He sorta took me aback when I first laid eyes on him. I mean, the guy looks like a schnauzer – how was I supposed to know it was a medical condition?

However, he was a quiet sort of kid, and after he showed me to my compartment on the train, he told me he was a big fan and that I shoulda won my fight with Fitzsimmons and if he ever saw Wyatt Earp – who had refereed that particular unfairness – he'd bite him on the ass.

Well, that kind of sentiment was endearing, so I gave him an autograph and a nickel, and after that, we were best pals. Stumpy introduced me to the rest of the gang and got me into the weekly poker game, which was nice because it meant I didn't have to clout nobody to prove I was worthwhile to sail with this particular crew. Old habits die hard, I guess.

I may have mentioned before that Larry the boss was something of a tightwad. I mean, I'm a penny pincher, myself, but this guy made me look like one of them Rockefellers. To make a long story short, the train was always breaking down for one danged thing or another.

We hadn't gone a hundred miles after we pulled out of Chicago when we had to stop because the engine was overheating. So we limped into a sleepy little town called Woodstock and proceeded to wake it up like it's never been woken up before.

Larry was busy trying to get the train repaired, so Jake Stein, our stage manager, scoured the town for a place to hole us up and maybe perform so we could pay for the repairs.

Woodstock had one of them old time theaters, the kind that used to be an opera house before the talking pictures came along. So, it had a screen that they could pull up and stow up in the rafters, and then you could put on a show. And that's just what we did.

For my part, I came out while Jake Stein narrated my particulars and I tore up playing cards and bent washers with my fingers and did a couple of muscle man poses. Stuff like that. They wanted me to talk about some of my great fights, and I admit, I was lousy at first. However, the Woodstock audience was pretty forgiving, and so before too long, I was living the high life again, which kinda rubbed some of the other acts the wrong way. The only one who stuck by me was Stumpy.

We weren't three days into our stay when the Gentleman Farmer's Commune blew into town for their monthly Trades Days appearance, and let me tell you, they took over the whole town square. Everywhere you looked there was livestock and fruits and vegetables and preserves and all manner of farming utensils and a bunch of stuff I didn't even know what it was. The rest of the town knew, and so did the neighboring towns and villages, because we were playing to packed houses after that, and we even doubled the number of shows we put on.

Larry was beside himself over our good fortune. He gave each of the acts two dollars and told us to hit the town, on him. I asked him for more money, but he said he needed it to pay for a replacement piston coming from Utica, New York, and I said with the number of hicks in town to see us, he had enough for two pistons and he could afford to give me a fin, and then he started to protest, so I lifted him off of his feet and shook him a little bit, and after that he coughed up three more bucks, so I let him go. Sometimes you just gotta be firm with your manager.

I hit the town and made sure to stop in all five speakeasies before deciding which one was my favorite. At each new watering hole, I found I had picked up some new followers, so when I ended up back at the White Orchid Tea Room with over twenty of my new best friends, we managed to chase out all of the respectable customers, and that meant the gambling could commence on the parlor tables instead of in the damp basement.

At some point, I remember being dared to see if I could knock out with a single blow one of the Gentleman Farmer's cows what were tethered outside. Turned out, it wasn't a cow, but a bull. Also, and I didn't know this at the time, but it's a lot harder to head butt a bull than you might think.

I woke up at sunrise with a splitting headache, half in and half out of a watering trough, and all hell breaking loose on the square. The Gentleman Farmers, many of whom apparently get up at the crack of dawn, were hollering and waving their arms about and crying bloody murder. I fixed my pants and wandered over to discover that someone had swiped six or seven chickens from Farmer Brinley, in the dead of night when no one was looking, and what kind of a town was the police chief running here, anyway?

Since it wasn't none of my business, I made my way back to the train, having no dough on which to spend for breakfast, and joined up with some of the other acts, straggling in and looking like they'd been trying to punch out cows, themselves.

I found Stumpy sleeping under my bunk, rousted him, and we went over to the depot for a ham steak breakfast. It was Stumpy's treat, since he hadn't spend any of his bonus money the night before. The waitress gave Stumpy one of those horrified looks I'd seen a few times in my life, but I told her to mind her P's and Q's and just keep the black coffee coming if she knew what was good for her.

Despite my defense of his peculiar visage, Stumpy wasn't too hungry so I finished off his ham steak, as well. Thus fortified, we ambled back to the train car in time to see Larry talking to the police chief and a clutch of Gentleman Farmers, all glaring at the train in a suspicious manner. Larry saw us coming and made a *get lost* gesture in between swinging his arms around.

Stumpy dragged me off to the far side of the train, away from the crowd, and we climbed on at the front of the passenger cars. I made my way back to where Larry was facing off the mob and peered down at the irate dirt pushers until Larry managed to convince them to go away.

"What's that all about?" I demanded as Larry climbed up into the train, mopping his brow.

"That cop was questioning us about some chickens that were stolen last night. You didn't see anything, did you?"

I told Larry that I been too tight to see anything except the inside of a water trough, and he told me he had no idea what I was talking about, but if I heard anything about the missing chickens, to tell him so he could take the heat off of us, and I told him I would. Then I crawled into my berth and slept until it was time for the show.

That night, we had another packed house, but it was a very different kind of audience. It seems that some of the Gentleman Farmers were of the opinion one of us was a chicken thief, so they showed up with pitchforks and tomatoes as a gesture of their displeasure.

I was ready to run out there and wade into them until the floor was knee-deep in gore, but Stein told me it was better to win them over with a good show than with a left hook.

I disagreed, of course, but let him have his way and it turned out, he was right. The rest of the gang gave those dirt eating yokels the show of their lives. A couple of lucky kids from the audience got to pull on Laslo Sanchez, our Fake India Rubber Man, and the Ling family set all of their hoops on fire for the little ones to jump through. The crowd ate it up, and not a single tomato was thrown, as a result.

The only one who seemed not so happy about the events was Stumpy. He just moped around backstage and worked the curtain and hauled stuff on and off the stage between acts. For a short guy, he's pretty strong.

I tried to ask him what was wrong a couple of times, but he just shook his head and kept on working. I didn't want to get between him and his job, so I left him alone.

After the show, Larry gathered us all up and said, "Look everyone, the Gentleman Farmer's Commune is still riled up about them chickens, so I think we should all go back to the train together and stay there for the night."

There were a couple of groans and mutters, but most everyone saw the logic of the request. So, we tromped down to the depot, in mass, and loaded onto the train, whereupon several poker games broke out and the Ling family passed around some of their private stock of Chinese hooch and got everyone pole-axed drunk. I passed out holding a seven high straight and hoping vaguely that Stumpy would look after my meager winnings.

I woke up suddenly when a brick came crashing in through the train window and hit me square in the back of the head. It woke me up, and it also shattered the brick into a bunch of pieces. This irritated me, because I knew Mama Ling would make me clean up the brick debris, which wasn't fair since I wasn't the one who threw it. I jumped up to see what was the matter and almost got another brick in the snoot for my troubles.

It was the Gentleman Farmer's Commune, but not any of them were acting very gentleman-like. They were banging on the train, smashing glass, and calling for our heads. They were yelling things like, "Chicken thief," and, "Lousy layabouts," and a few other things that weren't as polite. As you can imagine, I took grave exception to these insulting remarks, and I let fly a torrent of expressions and euphoniums I picked up in various saloons and boxing rings and ports of call over the years, and it was strong enough to blow the clod hopper's ears back and momentarily institute a cease fire on our poor dilapidated train.

By the time the Gentleman Farmers had regained their composure and was venturing to sally forth with another salvo, Larry and Jake had woke up and thrown on enough clothes to be presentable and they came running and inserted themselves between us and the mob. They were upset at being woke up before eleven o' clock on a Saturday, and I can't say I blamed them.

The local police showed up just as hostilities flared anew, and they managed to beat back the Gentleman Farmers long enough to get the story – more chickens was missing.

This time, it was over a dozen birds, and from two different farmers, no less. To make matters worse, whoever done it made a real mess of the coops and tore great gaping holes in the wood planks and in general ruining the chicken wire.

Farmers Gantrey and Snell were downright livid and demanding payment for their chickens and their coops. Immediately, Jake and Larry wanted to know how we came to be under suspicion, and the leader of the mob, Farmer Stebbins, triumphantly held up a chicken feather.

"Here, you perfidious cad!" he said with relish. "We followed the trail of feathers to here!" The certainty of his claim was enthusiastically voiced by the rest of the hoe-slingers, and it looked as if a new exchange of missile fire was about to occur.

That's when Larry stepped up and declared that if it would suit them, he and Farmer Stebbins would inspect the train, car by car, to find the missing chickens. Gantry and Snell hopped onto the train with Stebbins, and so I tagged along in case any of them got fresh.

We hadn't gone through three cars before we found Stumpy the Goon in the baggage car, tears in his eyes, a broom in one hand, and a dustbin in the other.

"I found these here," he said. "They were all over the floor, so I swept 'em up." He showed us. The dustbin was full of feathers.

Stebbins lunged at Stumpy and I checked him with an

outstretched arm. "Belay that act of violence," I growled. "He didn't do it. He found the feathers, and that was all."

Stumpy nodded furiously, but it was pretty clear no one but me believed him, not even Jake and Larry.

I asked Stumpy where he found the feathers, and he said they were all over the floor, starting at the door. We looked around a bit, but he'd done a real thorough job of sweeping up and there weren't any other chicken feathers to be found on anyone's belongings.

They kept looking for the chickens all throughout the train, with Larry and the farmers haggling like crazy over the cost of the birds and the coops. In the end, they found nothing, and Larry handed over a wad of cash to the disgruntled farmers that may have well been his left leg from the way he howled about it.

Afterward, he and Jake stood around, talking, casting meaningful glances over at Stumpy and me. I told Stumpy to stay close to me in case someone was to give him the business, and I'd protect him.

We didn't do much for the rest of the day. Everyone was mad at Stumpy because they thought he was eating the chickens, and Stumpy moping and crying didn't help matters none. I finally took him over to the theater early so we could get set up and he wouldn't have to interact with anyone from the show. There were a few glares and muttered comments from the Gentleman Farmers, but other than that, we was left alone.

Stumpy was already backstage when everyone showed up, and he stayed as far away from the gang as he could. Our crowd was low, owing much to the fact word had spread about our alleged chicken thievery and no one wanted to be entertained by a bunch of chicken thieves. We even brought up Colonel Strathmore's mummy box up from the train as an added attraction, and had some special handbills printed. No one cared. People are fickle.

As if that weren't bad enough, Larry pulled Stumpy over in the middle of my act and told him that he was gonna garnish his wages until the chickens were paid for, and what's more, with all of the abject hostility in the air, it would be better if he stayed in the theater overnight, to guard our meager possessions from diabolical sabotage or some such.

"Aw, Stumpy, quit cryin'," I said, as we moved Colonel Strathmore's mummy box back into the wings, it being considerably heavier than I remembered.

"But everybody hatesh me," said Stumpy in that weird little lisping voice of his. "I gotta weakness for yard bird, Tom, but I been on the wagon for schix months!" He looked at the ground, his cleft-like lip quivering. "Larry's gonna make me go back to the schircus. I don't wanna go back. I like it here. I get to wear pants."

He looked like he was gonna start blubbering again. I had to help him, but I didn't know what to do.

"Listen, Stumpy, here's the deal – I'll stay here with you, and we'll stay up all night, keeping an eye on one another. We'll just guard our stuff, here, in case those flop-wristed farmers try to muck about with our kit. In the morning, when more chickens are missing, they'll know it won't be you, because I'll have been with you here all night. And then you can get back into the show. How's that?"

Well, Stumpy was so grateful he nearly embraced me, but I deflected him and told him to wait here while I went and got us some sandwiches for the night.

When I came back with food and some snuck out booze, there was a cop waiting for us. "I gotta lock you in, Mr. Sharkey, on orders from the mayor."

"What?" I yelped. "Are we criminals or something?"

"It's the Gentleman Farmer's Commune," he said, quietly. "They wield considerable economic power in this county, and the whole city council is plumb scared of them." He stepped back out through the stage door and stuck his head in again. "Don't worry," he said. "I'll be right outside, all night. If you need something, just knock on the door and I'll do what I can for you."

I thanked the cop, for that was pretty reasonable, all things considered, and me and Stumpy sat down to our cold supper and played Slap Jack until the poor worried kid fell asleep in the remnants of his sandwich. I started drinking the hooch I'd snagged, and to my eternal chagrin, I fell asleep, too.

When I woke up, I thought at first I was back at sea and the giant squid was breaking up the ship. It was all crashing and splintering wood and someone shrieking, so I naturally ran to my post at the starboard side and fell off of the damn stage before I realized where I was. Stumpy ran over and helped me out of the front row and we raced back onto the stage, headed for the back door, and got there just in time to witness the carnage. The door had broken outward, into the side alley, in several large pieces and a large, dark, hulking shape, framed in the moonlight, tossed aside the bloody scantlings of our cop on guard. The bones clattered to the ground like a bag of marlin spikes, and Stumpy let out a mournful wail and ran as fast as he could in the other direction.

The shape turned at the sound, and damned if I wasn't staring into the not-so-withered face of Colonel Strathmore's mummy, now filled out and upright, walking about like it wasn't no big deal.

I tried to be diplomatic. "Liver Eatin' Johnson," I bellowed. "Get back in your bloody box this instant and quit making trouble for us. You owe Stumpy an apology, you big jackass!"

That didn't work quite like how I planned it out. His face squinched up, as if he was smelling his ownself, and he let out the most spine-tingling bellow I ever had the misfortune of hearing. Then he charged me like a blood-spattered looneytick.

I distinctly heard the word, "Injuns," come out of his ruined slit of a mouth, but then it opened to an unnaturally wide degree and after that, I was fighting a clutch of baseball bats in the midst of a cyclone.

His body was saturated from the blood of a boatload of chickens and one poor dumb idiot of a cop, but it was hard as spring steel and hurt like hell when he rained blows down upon my head and neck.

I punched him in the stummick and dang near broke my

hand. He did vomit up some of the claret he'd swallered earlier, so it was satisfying to know I could still hurt him.

I elected to dispense with the formalities of my former profession and proceeded to swing on him, free and generous, with all four of my appendages.

I quickly realized the error of my strategy.

What Liver Eatin' Johnson really wanted to do was bite my face off, and all I had done was bring myself well into biting distance. I had to move my head out of the way to avoid those jaws snapping shut like a bear trap and taking some of me with them. It wasn't long before he had me backed up into the wings, literally into the ropes that worked the scenery and the curtains and what not.

I bored in on Johnson, trying to connect a solid punch or two, but my flailing right got tangled up in the ropes and I had to dodge to get out of his way. I pulled my arm free just in time to avoid it getting bitten off, and what the dusty old fart got instead was a mouthful of rope. It snapped clean in two and dragged him up into the air about six feet as the *back flat* came thundering down.

As he was momentarily distracted, I seized the opportunity and grabbed his legs and heaved with all of my considerable might. Liver Eatin' Johnson let go of the rope with a venomous howl as I flung him across the floor, timing it just right to where the heavy scenery frame slammed down on his carcass and bisected him neatly in two.

You would have thought that wouldst stop him, but the topmost part of Liver Eatin' Johnson picked himself up on his hands and started stilt-walking in my general vicinity, barking obscenities.

I hauled back my boot to kick him in the mush when I was overwhelmed by no less than the gang from the train, the police force, and the Gentlemen Farmer's Commune, pouring into the theater like it was free beer night.

The farmers took one look at Liver Eatin' Johnson, now half

his stature, and made short work of him with their gardening implements. I'll never cross a farmer again after watching that spectacle, I can promise you.

The police spent the rest of the night grilling me and Stumpy about the Colonel and Liver Eatin' Johnson. The mummy box, they discovered, was full of chicken bones and chicken feathers. The farmers apologized to the two of us, and Larry and Jake gladly turned over Colonel Strathmore to the commune, who was fairly incensed at the damage done to his minion. Yeah, that's what he called it.

Seems Strathmore, who wasn't even really a colonel, by the way, was planning on building a brigade of dead historical figures to be used for some harebrained scheme involving soldiers and Fort Knox, whatever that is. After some general roughing up by the farmers, they turned him over to the police.

Once everything had settled down, I thanked Stumpy for mustering up the troops to help me, and he thanked me for sticking by him when the rest of the gang wouldn't.

I was a little banged up after fighting Liver Eatin' Johnson, so I spent a day recuperating in the train while they repaired it. Larry and Jake made sure me and Stumpy were well taken care of, if you know what I mean. And by that, I mean booze and women.

Turns out Larry managed to beat the cops back to the train and he riffled through Strathmore's luggage for his bankroll, which he used to pay himself back for the chickens and all of the damages, including a generous tip to himself on account of our mental anguish. And that's how Stumpy the Goon and me got to be such good pals.

# SAILOR TOM SHARKEY AND THE SOUTH SEAS CORMORANT

LOTS OF FOLKS ask me about my tattoo. Impressive, ain't it? This here's the kind of ship I used to sail on back when I was in the Merchant Marine. A four-masted schooner. We called 'em *windjammers* back then. I did a hitch in the Navy, which was pretty crazy to begin with, but nothing beats the wild times I had in the Merchant Marine. I joined up when I was twelve – had to lie about my age, o' course. Told 'em I was sixteen. They didn't believe me, but they didn't say no, neither.

I sailed out on the *Red Agnes*, and a more gangly, broken down, tub I've never seen. The crew matched the ship – beat up, half-starved, and mean as hell – but I was trying to get out of Dundalk and didn't have the means to choose my own way. I had to sail with any outfit that would take me.

We was shipwrecked four times trying to sail from Ireland to Australia, and then back up through the South Pacific islands. The first time was because we were doing thirty knots and the first mate was too drunk to notice we were heading right for an atoll. The second time was on account of a typhoon. The third time, we actually collided with another ship. As for the final time, well, that was my fault.

I ain't making no excuses, you understand. All I will say in my defense is I never steered a ship before, and apparently, you can do a lot of damage to a course heading in five minutes on open water.

I was a slip of youth, then, barely eighteen years old, and not in full control of my faculties and cunning, like now. So when the captain came back from the head to relieve me, he thought we were traveling in a north easterly direction, but we were headed due south, and none of us could check because the ship's dog had ate the compass the week before and we were up to our eyes in pea soup fog. The weather conditions didn't last more than an hour, but by then, we had sailed back into treacherous waters and *blam* goes the *Red Agnes* against the rocks. Nearly scuttled her, but good.

We all hopped out and tried to get the ship off the reef, but all we ended up doing was cutting ourselves up pretty good whilst the crew thought up new and ingenuous curses and oaths to hang on my ears.

Nothing worked. We were stuck until the storm let up, or the tide rolled in, or both, or neither. I can't remember exactly what was necessary to get us unstuck, because the captain ordered me into the drink to follow the sound of the surf so we could get on dry land.

I asked him why I had to go, and he said it's my fault we were stuck on these rocks because I couldn't steer a ship, and I told him it was really his fault for handing me the wheel and expecting me to not spin it a few times, and he said only an imbecile would spin a ship's wheel in a fog, and I told him I was not an imbecile, I was Irish, and he said what's the difference, and after that I sorta lost my temper and took a swing at the old man. I won't go into the details of what happened next, but when the entire crew threw me overboard, I figured I'd lost the argument and made for the beach as quickly as I could manage.

It wasn't a long swim, maybe a quarter of a mile or so, but in the dark, and in the fog, and with the crew's scandalous language raining down on me, and the storm raging, it felt a lot longer. But I got to the beach and took a little time dragging driftwood and leaves around, and kicking a rough sand pit into shape, because they didn't think to send the shovel overboard after me, and when I got it all piled together, I used a couple of wax-coated matches to light the fire, and soon it was crackling and smoking despite the rain and the wind. I managed to keep it going, and soon it was high enough for them to see. Even still, I made a couple of torches and waved the rest of the crew in, who all came ashore piled up in the longboats like cordwood.

The storm and the fog blew over in the middle of the night, leaving us wet and shivering on the beach. Some of the guys kept the fire going, while the captain kept peering out at the ship with his telescope and cussing to beat the devil. Everyone else was muttering and looking at me, so I made myself scarce.

I walked inland a bit, following what looked like a natural trail of sorts, and not a stone's throw away from the beach, I found this giant statue carved out of black rock.

It looked kinda like a man, only misshapen, like when you look into a funhouse mirror. But I honestly wasn't thinking too much about art appreciation because piled up around the base of the statue was literally mounds of food! Mostly fruits, but there was also dried and smoked fish and what looked like some lizard parts, and other sundries and strange looking vegetables.

We were all starving, though, so who cared if it was a little weird? I grabbed up an armful of vittles and ran back to the crew and yelled, "Hey, you lubbers! Who's hungry?"

Well, wouldn't you know it, I suddenly went from being a sheep-killing dog to everyone's best mate. I grabbed a couple of guys and we made off with the rest of the food. A few more men paddled back to the *Red Agnes* and liberated one of the ale casks, and we had a fine old time on the beach, singing shanties and dancing around the fire like kids until everyone passed out, fat, drunk, and happy.

Yeah, I might have messed us up temporarily, but in the end, I came through for my crew. Those thoughts lulled me into a gentle sleep, staring blissfully at the crackling fire.

Those comforting thoughts were chased away the next

morning, when we were awakened, at spear point, by a bunch of painted heathens. And let me be very clear about this – there are natives, and then there are heathens and savages.

We traded with the natives a lot. Sometimes it was food for liquor, or livestock for trinkets. We had a special crate or two at all times for when we were near a friendly island. They all had goofy names I could never pronounce, and they wore grass and scrap cloth and little else, but they were all right. Lots of singing and dancing to please their gods, or what-have-you. Natives.

Then there was these painted heathens. We ran into a few of them, too. Never happy to see us. Always shooting arrows at the ship, and chasing us out of the jungle. Some of them were cannibals, or so we thought, and some of them were just murderous, and hated sailors for some past indiscretion. We learned pretty quick to steer clear of those islands. But I guess this time, we didn't have much of a choice.

So, we wake up to spear points and shouting and scowling red faces with bones in their noses and weird swirls on their faces and some of them even had pointed teeth. They were tattooed all over, mostly naked, and they were madder than anyone I've ever seen.

Most of the boys had left their firearms on the ship, but more than a dozen brought their knives and machetes, which were brandished with enthusiasm, and it looked for a minute like we were going to meet our bloody end right there on the beach.

The captain finally intervened, and barked a few orders for everyone to hold off on the slaughter, and that's when one of the leaders stepped up – wearing more feathers and skins than the rest of them – and said a few words in English. The Captain nearly wept for joy as he tried to make friends with the fellow.

They weren't on a friend-making mission. It took a long time, and involved a lot of pointing and drawing pictures in the sand, but the upshot was this – someone took their sacred offering to their heathen island god, who lived up on the volcanic mountain in the distance.

Yeah, alright, it was all of that food I discovered.

Once the truth came out, I went back to being a sheep-killing dog in the eyes of the crew, but look at it from my side – I'd seen altars and offering bowls and sacred rocks on a dozen or more of these backwater mud holes, and they all had fruit, or a goat, or something like that to offer up to the gods, and let me tell you, nine times out of ten, it was the old medicine man himself who snuck out in the dead of night and ate the food, or let the goat go, or whatever was necessary to keep the peasants from revolting. So, how was I to know that they would be so touchy about it? I was just being the right hand of fate, trying to help keep up the moral fiber of the ignorant savages, and this is the thanks I get.

The spear points weren't being stowed away during all of this parlay. In fact, the natives were getting more and more bent out of shape. After a fashion, the captain and the decorated fellow, who was apparently the tribe's big kahuna, could conversate reasonably well, and it turns out, there was a time limit to this offering being paid off, or the god, who was called Maho, would visit upon them in great anger and eat all of the children in the village.

The natives were pretty upset by that idea, and I can see their point. Trading babies for bananas seemed like a bad bargain to me, but you have to remember these Islanders don't get out very much.

Once the captain got the lay of the land, he started grinning and said he had the perfect solution – they could have me! The crew liked this idea a lot, but the natives weren't convinced.

Now, remember, I was a lad at the time, but even though I was youthful, six years of daily beatings, weekly fisticuffs amongst the crew, and regular instruction on the scientific art of pugilism had turned me into a trim engine of destruction.

I always was barrel-chested, but there wasn't an ounce of fat on me. My fists were toughened by years of salt water, my hide was like sharkskin, and my punches couldst dent battleship steel.

I was pretty sure the captain meant to maroon me, but I stepped up and said, "I'll be yer champion, if that's what you need. Your god won't eat no children as along as Thomas J.

Sharkey is on watch!"

The captain translated, and the first mate was shaking his head sorrowfully, but the natives all dropped their spears and arrows and give a great big cheer.

I was in! They crowded around me, patting me on the back and touching my close-cropped hair. The first mate pushed his way through the admirin' throng and dressed me down. "You knucklehead! There ain't no Maho, and so there ain't nothing for you to punch out, and so what are you gonna do?"

"Relax," I said, tapping me temple. "I got it all figured out. Whatever is eating their food is probably a monkey or a panther or something entirely natural. I figure, I'll wait up in the trees with a pistol and shoot the beast when it comes to collect."

"Keep thinking, genius," said the first mate. "What are you gonna do when the natives see whatever you shot?"

"Easy," I said. "I'll hide the carcass, and tell the natives that I scared their mountain god off. Then we'll take the body out to sea so they will never find it. Trust me, it'll work!"

The first mate was shaking his head again. He always did that whenever I was around. "You know, it's childlike enough you may just get away with it." He handed me his pistol and holster. "Here. I'll come collect it before they cremate you. You do know which end the bullets come out, right?"

I ignored his insult, because at the moment, I was the subject of some sort of dispute between the chief and the kahuna. It all stemmed from the fact I was not a member of the tribe, and in their eyes, I was a naked savage because I had no tattoos, Well, there was no way I was going to let them draw spirals and swirls on my face, and I started to say so, but the kahuna intervened and said they would paint me with berries and dyes, and if I lived, they would make me a member of their tribe.

I asked the captain if he translated that right, and he said, "Yeah, if you live, Sharkey. And right now, I've got two bucks says this hunk of rock is where you cash in your chips."

"I'll take that action," I told him. "You owe me a week's wages anyway from last month. I'll put it up that I make it through the night."

This started a large betting pool, with the crew all placing bets on how I'd meet my end, and if it would involve the kahuna strangling me in my sleep.

I had ten bucks riding on my staying alive, so I went back to the statue in the clearing to scout it out and look around. Anything to increase my odds.

Back in the clearing, I was by myself, and I had a chance to study this Maho up close. I don't know if you've ever been to Easter Island, but this statue in the clearing looked a lot like those heads. Only, instead of a head, it was a whole body. One guy, standing about seven or eight feet tall, carved out of glassy black rock. Some of the edges were sharp as a knife. Grossly misshapen.

It kinda reminded me of the stories my grannie told me about giants in the hills when I was younger. She could spin a yarn, and her depictions of the giants and the ogres and their goings-on used to curl my hair.

I was ruminating on all of this when one of my fellow sailors, another Irish mate by the name of O'Brien, found me and struck up conversation.

"You know, all betting aside, we're all in a bit of bother, here."

"How do you mean?" I asked.

"Well, think on this way – what happens if you win?"

"I expect they'll let us camp out on the beach until we can get the ship off the rocks and repaired."

"Aye," he said, nodding in agreement. "And what happens if you lose? If you can't produce this Maho, or worse, nothing ever shows up?"

I hadn't considered that. He let the implications of our dire predicament sink in.

"Holy Hell!" I kicked the sand. "This is a jam-up, but good."

O'Brien nodded again. "Look, I got an idee…suppose we set a trap? I mean, if it's an animal, you need all the help you can get. Everyone knows you're a lousy shot."

"What do you have in mind?"

O'Brien pulled me into the middle of the clearing. "How about this: Whist you're in the village getting all painted up, me and a few of the boys will sneak over here and dig a pit, see?" He drug his foot in the sand, making a rough square around us, about ten feet on each side. "Not too deep, but deep enough. We'll put some netting down below, and then we'll cover it up with leaves. When the critter comes into the clearing, looking for food, it'll stumble into here, and you can shoot him and haul him up in the net. Quick-like, see? That way, he can't get away if you miss."

"O'Brien, you're a genius," I said. "You can plan my battle strategy anytime."

"Okay, then," he said. "Go up to the village and get ready. Take your time, see? Don't come back here until after it's dark. We'll have it all set up for you."

My head was bristling with all of this strategy as I made my way up the path and into the village. The captain and the kahuna had gotten pretty chummy by this time, and were talking and smoking as I approached. "Tom," the captain said, all smiles. "Come here and listen to the plan!"

"More plans?" I didn't think my brain could hold so much stuff at once.

"Aye, and listen up! They're gonna paint your useless hide from stem to stern in some sort of heathen ceremony. I think it's a sacrament, or something to that effect. Anyway, they want you to wait at the statue when the moon is highest in the sky."

"Aw, I was gonna do that anyway, Captain," I said. The kahuna clapped his hands and yelled something, and then all at once, I was surrounded by five beautiful island girls. Well, maybe this wouldn't be so bad after all, I mused, as they led me away, giggling.

Well, they got me into this hut that smelled more like a kitchen than a boudoir, and they took off my raggedy shirt and my breeches and had me nearly naked as the day I was born, and no sooner than I began to entertain some conjugal thoughts, but they started slapping a lot of oils, and juices, and goo of all sorts on me.

It all smelled pretty good, like what you'd sop a pig with before you roast him, and I asked them if they were going to draw anything on me, because they all seemed more interested in rubbing in the sticky pineapple juice and squirting limes in my hair. When they got through with me, I smelled like a Hawaiian Luau and looked like I'd just come out of a three day bender.

They walked me back over to the fire, and commenced to feeding me like a king. I ate all manner of wild game, fruits, some vegetables, and had about six or eight coconut shells worth of some strong, sour, alcoholic swill they brewed up themselves. But boy, did it do the trick! We were all singing, and they were dancing around me, and every one of the girls came over and kissed me on the cheek or the forehead. I never felt so grand in all my life.

At last, the kahuna called everybody quiet. He stood me up, and not too steadily, for I'd had a few more cups of their home brew and it was having an effect on my sea legs.

He said something to me in his jibber-jabber, and I told him he was an all right guy for a heathen and a cannibal, and everyone cheered. The kahuna then turned me around and the whole tribe marched me out to the edge of the forest, where the trail to the clearing starts, and they actually sang me goodbye as I staggered down the path.

The night air was cool and crisp, like most tropical ports, and you'd never have known that just the last night it was a raging squall and heavy fog to vex poor sailors. Fickle place, the South Pacific.

I turned off the path and entered the clearing and was dismayed to notice the place had been trashed. There were giant leaves and palm fronds everywhere.

The clearing was not like this when I left it, and I let fly a few colorful oaths as I gathered up an armful of the flotsam to clear the way for whatever was coming. And that's when I remembered, about two footsteps too late, that all of the leaves were supposed to be there because they were hiding an enormous excavated pit. I had plenty of time to remember the conversation with O'Brien as I fell, head first, into the giant hole.

Cursing anew, I stood up and took stock of myself. I had a lump on my head, but it wasn't even close to the biggest lump I ever had, so I figured I was all right. I grabbed hold of the net to hoist myself up, and only succeeded in pulling the weighted end down on my head.

Another lump quickly formed on the other side of my head, and so I decided not to try that trick again. The pit wasn't too deep, maybe eight feet or so, but to I guy with not a lot of northerly reach, it was a pain in the butt. I jumped up a few times, just in case I could make it, and on the third time I got my fingers clamped onto the side, but the sand disintegrated under my weight and I fell back down into the pit. I was stuck until someone or something came along.

I'd always heard the expression *be careful what you ask for*, but I never understood it until I was in that pit and I heard someone walking, crunching and crashing through the leaves, and I started yelling, "Hey, I'm down here!' not thinking it might be unwise to do such a thing.

Their homemade liquor had dulled my analytical thinking, but good. I saw a shadow fall across the pit in the moonlight, and then suddenly, the sky was falling.

I'm not kidding around, neither. For a second, I couldn't see anything but something huge, dark, and heavy collapsing on me. It was a man, only, it wasn't. I mean, it was a man, except for two things. One, he was at least seven feet tall and two, he looked exactly like the statue.

It was Maho! In the flesh, no less. He made an inarticulate bellow as he scrambled to his feet in the pit. When he stood up, he was able to see over the edge of the pit. And his proportions were all screwy, just like that statue, right down to the high forehead and wide, sloping chin that resembled a cow-catcher on a steam engine. He was just as surprised at falling in the pit, and seeing me, as I was at seeing him.

Maho finally assessed the situation. He lunged for me and scooped me up in his two hands, holding me just like a hoagie. He sniffed me, and I heard his stummick gurgle, and I had a recollection about how delicious I smelled earlier and then it all sorta fell into place – this giant had plans to make hash out of me.

Thankfully, I had enough oils and goo on me to get one arm free. It was the worst punch I ever threw, because it had none of my weight behind it, but I clocked him one right on the beak and he howled and dropped me. I landed and went into a tuck and roll and scooted through his legs. When I popped up on the other side, I spun around and before the giant could adjust his stance, I went to work on his kidneys with a series of rabbit punches delivered at full force.

When he did turn around, it was faster than I expected. His sweeping left crashed into the side of my head and for a minute I was seeing stars. He outweighed me by about two hundred pounds if he weighed an ounce. But six years aboard the *Red Agnes* taught me how to throw a punch and also how to take one. Daily bullying. Daily beatings. And now this big, dumb lubber wanting to eat me for supper. Enough was enough!

I crouched and ducked his swinging reach, moving inside and hammering away at his bread basket. I couldn't tell if I was hurting him or not, but I knew if I did enough damage it would weaken him. Just like the wind and the surf, pounding away on our ship. Eventually the wood and iron would warp and break. But I wouldn't give up. I had to beat him down if I wanted to leave this pit alive.

Maho roared and kept trying to scoop me up again, presumably for a hug or a bite. Every time he lowered his head, I whaled on his nose or cracked him on the ear, which sent him howling and retreating. Then he'd charge me and the dance would begin anew. I don't know how long we circled and dove and lunged in that cramped and crowded pit, but I was beginning to get tired.

More than once Maho got one of his biscuit hooks on me and I had to pry myself loose before he could do any more damage. I caught a glimpse of his teeth in the moonlight – sharp as a killer whale's, they were, and he had a mouth full of 'em.

In my delirium, I imagined I was back on the ship, in the crew's quarters, with their voices ringing out as I gave the latest bully the works. For once, the crew was cheering my name instead of running me down. I smiled out of sheer giddy exhaustion and that's when Maho's right hand shot out and wrapped itself around my neck.

He lifted me up and I felt my legs dangling in space. The air was clouding up. I was low on breath. I could hear the shouts of my mates turn to the howls from Davy Jones' Locker. But if I was going to cash in my chips, I would make sure Maho anted up, too.

I grabbed his wrist with both arms and hoisted myself up and wrapped my legs around his forearm and proceeded to cling to him like a barnacle. Using my legs for leverage, I got my neck free of his grip and then I turned his thumb over and broke it with a satisfying snap.

Maho howled and screamed and tried to shake me loose, but I had a hold him now, and wasn't inclined to let go. He tried to pull me off using his good hand, and I took advantage of his efforts to kick him in mush. Another crack told me his nose broke, and the claret flowed forth in red ribbons.

Maho crouched down to use his foot to scrape me off, but before he could do so, I transferred my hold from his arm to his enormous neck. It took some grappling, and I caught a few more good blows before I was able to get both legs around his neck. There I was, hanging upside down on this South Pacific giant like an Irish necktie. I could barely clasp my feet together, but I squoze for all I was worth.

Maho dropped to one knee and I reached out with my arms and pushed against the side of the pit, straining to topple him. Something had to give, and it wasn't going to be me!

Finally, I heard Maho groan. He tried to stand up, but merely listed to one side. With all the strength left in him, he flung himself forward and we crashed into the pit wall. He had me pinned, and my ears were ringing, but he was sagging. His shoulders dropped and he fell away from me and collapsed in an untidy heap. I had beaten him.

But the effort took its toll, I can tell you. I felt lightheaded, and my breathing was difficult because that last tumble cracked a couple of ribs. Also, my right arm wasn't working so good. I was in worse shape than I thought because I felt like I was floating out of the pit and out into the open air and the rosy fingers of dawn stinging my swollen eyes. I heard O'Brien say, "Hail Mary, and Joseph, he's alive!" Then I passed out for good.

I came to in a native hut. My wounds had been tended and my shoulder popped back into its socket. Instead of smelling like a suckling pig, they had smeared me with some horrible-smelling sticky mud they insisted was good medicine because, after all, I woke up, didn't I?

I didn't have the heart to tell them I was endowed with a prolific constitution and let them keep to their heathen ways. At least they weren't eating me or the crew.

The captain explained everyone heard the crashing and witnessed the battle. The natives weren't angry at me kayoing their mountain god. Some of the story got lost in the translation. Maho was not their god, but rather one of their god's children, and a mischief-maker, at that. It turned out he'd been holding the village hostage for years. In the end, just another bully.

The natives suddenly took a different outlook on us, and while I was laid up, they helped get the *Red Agnes* off the rocks and more or less seaworthy again.

Out of thanks for sticking up for them, they made me an honorary member of the tribe. The also insisted on giving me a tattoo. I told 'em not to put any of their backward markings on me, but to give me something I could appreciate.

So, with O'Brien's help, the old kahuna gave me this ship on my chest – the *Red Agnes* – and at the insistence of O'Brien, the legend above it. I asked O'Brien about the words after admiring the work in the mirror.

"You don't remember?" he asked. "Boy, you must've been pretty well gone. That's what you kept saying when you were beating down that giant. 'I'll never give up the ship!' You just kept saying it over and over. When we hoisted you out of the pit, you were still muttering it."

I truthfully don't remember it that way, but it's become something of a trademark for me. And it became our rallying cry whenever the crew needed some extra incentive.

I took it with me to the Navy, which came in handy when we had to fight off those mechanical monsters in the Persian Sea. But that's another story, for another time. The best part of all of that business was this – I won the bet!

The crew had to fork over all of their dough, and I spent the rest of our hitch loaning other sailors their own money back for booze and loose women.

# SAILOR TOM SHARKEY AND THE CHRISTMAS SAVAGES

I WAS FEELING pretty low in December, 1914. Kate was gone, and I was all alone, and it just wasn't feeling much like Christmas, what with everything going on. Bar troubles, gang troubles, political troubles, you name it, I had it. I'd even managed to work up a good-sized gambling debt, betting on the horses. Not a very merry Christmas, I can tell you that for sure.

I mostly kept to myself, but even loners get thirsty, so I spent some time in the bar, sipping whisky and eating pickled eggs. It was no kind of lunch or dinner, but with Kate gone, I didn't have the energy for much else.

It was in this general state of configuration that Charlie Murphy came walking into the bar, his nose up, his eyes all crinkly, like he was smelling something bad. Politics, most likely. Murphy was the leader of Tammany Hall, which meant he controlled the Gas Light District, and it also meant he controlled me. At least, he thought he did. Or, more appropriately, I thought he didn't.

Anyway, he comes walking in and gives me that stiff-upper lip look, and holds out a beefy hand, and says, "Tom, how're you doin', lad?" He was peering at me over the tops of his eye glasses, which made him look like a scolding Bishop.

"Getting along, Charlie," I replied. "Buy you a soda?"

"I'll pass," he said, his expression unchanged. Teetotaler, he was, and he was a professional at it, to boot. An Irish teetotaler. That's practically unchristian. "Listen, Tom, I know you're stretched thin right now, and I've got a wee favor to ask that can put you right again."

There wasn't much Charlie Murphy didn't know, and I resented him keeping tabs on me like he did. Then again, I knew he kept tabs on most of the Irish celebrities in town. Political insurance, he once called it. That and his *wee favors*.

I finished my whisky and signaled Prong-Head for another one. "Not another political appearance? Election season is November, Charlie."

"This one's different," Murphy said. "Personal appearance. An orphanage. St. Ignatius' Home for Wayward Souls," he smiled, indulgently. "You'll be the guest of honor. And I'll pay you fifty bucks."

"Remember when I used to get a thousand clams, just for walking in the door?" I asked.

"Those days are long gone, Tom. Ye've only got your reputation, now. So, what do you say? It's for the children."

I just knew he was setting me up for something, and I told him so, and he said, no, he wasn't, and so I said, what's the catch, and he said, he'd have some of the boys with me to pass out literature for Tammany Hall, and otherwise all I had to do was hand out presents and make a quick fifty bucks, which didn't begin to cover my debt, but I told him okay, anyway, because fifty bucks is fifty bucks.

It was only after I said yes that he started piling on the conditions. "So, I'll bring the Santa Claus suit over to you later today..."

"Belay that," I said. "Santy Claus? I can't be no Santy Claus."

Murphy looked shocked. "Why on Earth not?"

"Just look at me, Charlie. I ain't got the circumference to pull it off."

"There's padding in the suit, Tom," he explained in that convalescing way of his that always made me want to sock him.

"And a beard," he added, cutting short my next objection. "Don't worry, lad. It's the full package."

"I still don't think it'll work," I grumbled.

"Well, that's as may be, but I'll bet the kids will be so distracted by what we're bringin' 'em they won't even notice you're not the genuine article." He smiled, and clapped me on the back. "You're doin' the Lord's work," he said.

"Don't think so much o' yourself," I replied. He let that go and left me to my pickled eggs.

A couple of hours later, one of Murphy's cronies brought a large package which turned out to be my Santa suit. I tried it on, and after I rolled up the cuffs on the jacket and the pants, I gotta admit, I looked a lot like the Old Gent.

"Haw, haw, haw," I said, and the crony pointed out it's actually "Ho, ho, ho."

I told him I can't laugh like that because I'll sound stupid and besides, these kids won't know the difference no how. He gave me a look and was about to say something when a blast from a truck horn told us it was time to make the gig. He handed me an envelope with five tens in it, and I stuck the money down into my boot for safekeeping.

Seamus McInnery was driving the truck, and he give me a big hello when I jumped up into the cab. We talked about boxing as he drove the truck up the narrow streets. The other crony, who introduced himself as Duffy, just sat there and smoked. During a natural pause in the conversation, I remarked, "This is an awfully big truck for a bunch of presents for orphans. What're you givin' 'em, anyway?"

Duffy grinned and Seamus laughed. "Oh, there's a buncha dolls for the girls and baseball gloves and balls for the boys, but that's not what's in the truck," Duffy said.

"Okay, then, what's in the truck?"

Duffy started chuckling. "Charlie didn't tell 'im," he said to Seamus.

"No, he didn't," Seamus said. Catching my murderous look,

he wiped the smile off his face and said, "Tammy."

"Stop the goddamn truck!" I bellowed.

"Aw, Tom, don't be like that," said Seamus. "Think of the children."

"Yeah, Tom," said Duffy. "They're countin' on an appearance from Santa. You wouldn't want to disappoint a whole orphanage, now, would you?"

"You put me on the bill with a live tiger!" I hollered. "I don't play second fiddle to jugglers, because I can't do it myself, women who sing in real high voices, because it makes my teeth hurt, and any animal bigger than a dog! And Charlie knows it!"

"Tom, calm down, for Pete's sake!"

"I've been shanghaied by politicos! Now, let me out or I'll cream the insides of this truck with your whisky-soaked brains!"

Duffy started to talk some more, but Seamus motioned him quiet and pulled the truck over to a stop in front of a large church. "Okay, Tom, here you go." He set the brake and opened his door. "Come on out, Sailor Tom Sharkey!"

"Well, finally, Seamus, you're showing the proper feudal spirit..." I slid out of the truck and jumped to the ground, and landed right in the grip of a stooped-over old priest with glasses so thick I could've ice skated on them.

"Oh, Tom Sharkey! Bless me, St. Peter, I can die now and go to heaven! It's really you!"

"Yuh...yuh..." I tried to say something, but the old hymn flinger bowled right over me.

"When they told me this year we'd get a visit from St. Nicholas, and not only that, but it was the world-famous Tom Sharkey, I knew my prayers had been answered!" He grabbed my hand in his, and it felt like I was holding an assortment of chopsticks.

"Father Gilligan, Mr. Sharkey. And may I say, I've been a fan of yours ever since you set foot in San Francisco, lo, these many years back. I listened to all of your fights on the radio and I even waved at you during the St. Patrick's Day parade after your fight with Jeffries, and son, you looked right at me and waved back!"

I stood dumbfounded in the wake of all these personal revelations. I've heard people gush before, and I've talked to priests, but this was new to me. Most religious types throw up a crucifix when they see me, boxing being what it is.

"It's nice to meet you, Father," I said, retrieving my right mauler. "Now, if you'd be so kind as to call me..." That was about as far as I got when an unpleasant thought stole over me. "Say, what's the name of this church, anyhow?"

"St. Ignatius' Home for Wayward Souls," said Father Gilligan, beaming with pride. "And a more spirited and enthusiastic lot of children you'll never meet!"

I turned in a wrath on Duffy and Seamus, but they just pushed a giant bag of toys into my hands and said, "Come on, Santa. You're up, first. We'll bring the tiger out after you. First billing, and all that." Duffy smiled at me, and I made the instant determination that after this job was over, he'd be the one I punched first, even though Seamus was the one who played that dirty trick on me.

"All right, you thick-headed Micks," I growled, "Get in there and help me distribute this loot."

"Why, sure thing, Santa," said Duffy, and then he laughed.

Seamus held the door open and I stalked through it with Gilligan following after me, blathering away like his life depended on it.

Gilligan led me down a hallway and into a small choir room. "Now, the children are all inside the chapel," he explained, motioning to the door to the right. "I'll go around the long way, and come in from the other side. You listen at the door, here, and then I'll introduce you."

"Okay, then what?"

"Well, you'll come out and wish the children a Merry Christmas and maybe say a few things about how they have all been good little boys and girls. You know, be Santa Claus. Then we'll distribute the presents and you'll wish every boy and girl

Merry Christmas. Can you do that?"

"Merry Christmas," I repeated. "Yep. Merry Christmas!"

"Good," said Father Gilligan. He stepped around me and nearly sprinted out the door, looking like a question mark with legs. I checked my hat and my beard in the mirror, and pushed on the padding a little bit, just to make sure I was appropriately jolly. Then I heard through the door, "Say Hello to Father Christmas!"

I looked around. Father Christmas? Was this a variety show? Who the hell was that? I thought I was going on first? The kids were clapping and yelling, but I couldn't hear the opening act. Then they died down and Father Gilligan said, again. "Father Christmas!"

More clapping and shouting. Then nothing. I leaned in on the door, listening for Father Christmas, but couldn't hear anything. Maybe it was a deaf-mute show.

"Hello? Santa Claus?" It was Father Gilligan.

"I'm in here!" I bellowed.

"Will you come out and greet the children?" He sounded upset.

"Okay," I said. I threw open the door and strolled out onto the raised area where Father Gilligan stood. "Haw, haw, haw!" I said.

The children were quiet. They were all looking at me, their eyes wide. Maybe fifty of them in all, some of them real small and a few looking like teenagers. They just stared at me.

"Merry Christmas!" I said.

I couldn't understand it. No reaction. Weren't children supposed to love Santa Claus? It was a loveless room I was in, that's for sure.

"Er, Santa, was there something you wanted to say to the children?" Father Gilligan prompted.

"Oh, yeah. Merry Christmas!"

"Was there anything else?" he said, pointedly.

"Um...Merry Christmas?"

A little kid in the front row, maybe eight or nine, said, out loud, "Last year's Santa was a lot taller."

"And fatter," said the kid next to him.

Now the old bead-counter was getting flustered. "Have the children all been *good* this year?" he asked.

"Merry Christmas!" I said. I could tell he wanted me to say something else, but for the life of me, I didn't know what. And I couldn't stop saying "Merry Christmas," either. It was like being on the Ferris wheel at Coney Island. It's fun until you get up to the top, and then you get all woozy, and then you come down, but then you go right back up again.

I could feel my face getting red, and I was two seconds away from tearing these false riggings off, when Seamus and Duffy appeared behind me and said, "Okay, kids, who wants a present from Santa?"

The children all made shuffling motions and began filing dutifully up the stairs to receive their handouts. Every time I handed the kids their present, I said, "Merry Christmas," and after a while, the kids were saying it, too.

Some of them said it before I said it, and some of them said it at the same time I said it, and some of them just chuckled as they snatched their ill-gotten loot out of my hands. None of them said thank you.

A few of them tried to start a ruckus by pulling on my beard, or telling me I wasn't the real Santa. I threatened that kid with a beating and Father Gilligan pulled him aside when he started crying. The fellows were looking at me like I'd done something wrong, but it wasn't my fault the kid couldn't be civil, was it?

Eventually, we got the presents distributed, and Seamus and Duffy were throwing Tammany Hall buttons and hats out at the kids. Father Gilligan held his hands up for quiet and I took the cue and said, "And so, children, let this be a lesson to ya. Be good and kind and Santa will bring you stuff. But act up and cause a fuss and Santa may just hand you a beating! Merry Christmas!"

Father Gilligan's mouth was moving, but nothing was coming out. Duffy and Seamus were nowhere to be found. The kids were all looking at me, suspicious-like. What a bunch of ungrateful savages. All dressed up in their orphan clothes, looking at me like I was some sort of monster. Who brought them presents? Me, that's who.

Finally, Gilligan found his voice. "Let's thank Santa, children," he said in that prompting way grown-ups talk to kids. The little savages started clapping, feebly.

I heard that one kid in the front say, "Short and dumb. Some Santa Claus." I started for him, but Father Gilligan pushed me back into the choir room.

"I've an idea," he said. "Why don't you change into your regular clothes, and then we'll introduce you to the children so they will know who you really are? I think that would explain a lot," he said.

"Fine by me, Father," I said. I was tired of playing Santa, anyway.

Gilligan hurried back out into the chapel, and I looked around for my clothes only to remember I didn't bring any spare duds with me. Resigned to my fate, I sat down in on a piano stool and took off the hat and beard so I could catch a breeze. Then I heard an eruption the likes of which nearly knocked me off my stool. The kids were going nuts.

I went to the door and opened it a crack. Sure enough, there was Duffy, standing in front of a tiger cage that just barely enclosed Tammy, the official mascot of Tammany Hall.

She was just a cub when they got her, maybe a dozen years ago. They took her to all of the rallies and political fund-raisers, and she got pretty used to crowds of people. But that was then. Now she was older, and a lot crankier. But they still kept wheeling her out for public events. They just made sure she was well fed, first.

Well, Duffy was standing there, telling the children all about Tammy, and what kind of tiger she was, and how much she ate, and stuff like that. And, get this, the kids were eating it up! Some days, it doesn't pay to be me.

Duffy was explaining Tammy wasn't feeling too well, but if the kids wanted a closer look, they could form a line and each child could come stand by him and that way they could see Tammy real good.

Those kids got into line like they were being horse-whipped, each one pushing and poking someone else, jockeying for position. I watched as, one by one, they approached the spot where Duffy was, turned pale, and then quickly walked away. But they seemed to like it, too. Maybe that's what was missing in my Santa act — an element of danger.

I was mulling over the prospects of who someone like Santa Claus could fight when I noticed a small girl, one of the little brats who questioned my authenticity, was staring at the tiger with a strange little smile on her face.

She stepped closer to the cage, and Duffy, thinking she was fleeing the scene, motioned for the next kid to come up. But she didn't turn and go the way the rest of the children. Instead, she spun and headed for the back of the cage, on the opposite side.

Tammy's tail was sticking out of the cage bars, flicking to and fro, lazily. She stood there, apart from the rest of the group, staring at it like she was in a trance. "He's not sick," she finally pronounced. "He just wants to play." And so saying, she reached out and grabbed Tammy's tail with both hands and pulled like she was fishing for marlin.

A few things happened all at once. Gilligan, finally seeing where his young charge was, screamed "No, Mary Alice!"

Then Duffy, who saw what Gilligan saw, said a word you're not supposed to say in church.

Tammy, who was just minding her own business, roared and kicked both of her legs backward and pretty much shattered the cage door.

The children, upon hearing the roar and the crash, screamed bloody murder as a group, and, boy, did that upset Tammy, who wasn't used to such goings on. She gave a little jump, and then the top of the cage sorta buckled, and the next thing you know, there was a tiger loose in the church.

Tammy leapt out of the ruined cage and landed in a full stretch that looked an awful lot like she was fixin' to pounce on the little girl who'd done the tail pulling.

Father Gilligan was hollering bloody murder, trying to get Mary Alice to run to the edge of the platform whilst the rest of the kids ran like hell for the doors in the back of the chapel. Mary Alice, in fact, was the only thing in the room not moving. She stood there, eyes locked on Tammy. I could see the muscles in the big cat's back legs bunching up.

"Aw, hell," I said, and bolted out of the door onto the stage. I had enough time to do one really stupid thing. So, just as Tammy's back legs left the ground, I grabbed her tail with both hands and jerked her back down to the ground, away from the girl.

As the cat yowled in pain, I skidded to a stop in front of Mary Alice and kicked her in the direction of Father Gillian. She howled too, but I had my eyes on Tammy and, strangely enough, she had hers on me.

"Santa Claus kicked my bottom!" Mary Alice bellowed. "I just wanted to pet the big kitty! He's so mean!"

That was too much for me. I whipped around and said, "Listen here, you little biscuit-grabbing..."

The children screamed again, and this time, I knew why. I spun back around, but Tammy was in mid-air.

I tried to put my guard up, but my arms got tangled up in the floppy Santa suit, and by then, I felt all five hundred pounds of that mangy tiger slam me into the wooden floor like I was a paper doll.

My hands were on her throat, holding her head away from my neck, but her front and back claws were just gutting the Santa suit, literally. Stuffing flew everywhere, and I dimly heard the children scream, "The kitty's killing Santa!" I'm still not sure if they were horrified or cheering the cat on. Either way, the padded suit was the only thing that saved my life.

I finally got a leg up under Tammy's ribcage and kicked her

off of me. She tumbled once and then righted herself with a snarl, and I knew I was in for the fight of my life.

"Come on, Tom!" shouted Father Gilligan.

"Get the kids outta here!" I yelled back. "If she's tangling with me, then she can't eat any of your little savages."

"Tom, don't be stupid!" yelled Seamus. "Duffy's got a tranquilizer gun. He's getting it right now!"

"You don't be stupid!" I said. Tammy was coiling up for another leap at me. "She's gonna kill us all before that dumb Mick gets back!"

However, the blow she got was enough to knock me down and she lunged for me. I gave her a mouthful of boot in return, and Tammy stripped it off my leg like a fat man eating chicken. In a second, she'd destroyed the boot, and I took that second to get back on my feet.

Tammy smelt the blood, and she regrouped, licking her lips. I was in trouble. She circled me, slowly, and I tried to keep facing her while holding my cuts together with one hand.

That wasn't going to work real well. One more leap and I was done for. So, I abandoned the defensive posture, which was never my style, anyway, and squared off. Tammy made a hissing sound in her throat. She gathered herself up on her haunches and launched at me like an orange striped cannonball.

I had my fists up and cocked, and I met her in mid-air with a swing that had every ounce of my beef behind it. My whole arm went numb, but I heard a thunderous crack and Tammy gave a most peculiar yowl and dropped to the ground. Damned if I didn't knock her out! She keeled over like she'd been pole-axed, and I felt a little sorry for her. I mean, she was just doing what came natural, after all. And would it have been so bad if she'd eaten a couple of the orphans?

Duffy and Seamus ran up around this time, and while Seamus dragged me off the stage and away from the cat, Duffy wept and howled bloody murder that he was gonna kill me. I stood up and told him to bring his lunch, and also that rifle, because he was gonna need it. Then the blood loss sorta got to me, along with all the beer I'd drunk, and I sorta passed out.

And that was pretty much that.

They moved me to Father Gilligan's office and I laid there, bleeding out, until the sawbones arrived and proceeded to stitch me back together again. Duffy and Seamus doped up the tiger and took her to the zoo, where they told them she was concussed, but with some care and attention, she'd make a full recovery.

They did give Duffy a hard time because he shouldn't own a tiger, and on account of the fact she was pretty old and didn't have a proper diet. Duffy cried like a little girl and swore he'd do better.

Naturally, Murphy blamed me for the whole thing, like it was my idea to introduce a tiger to a bunch of feckless orphans. He demanded I pay for the tiger, and I told him to go pound salt up his nose and pay for my medical bills, instead.

And that pretty much ended my association, if there ever really was one, with Tammany Hall. What Murphy did to me later, I'm sure had everything to do with me breaking his prize tiger. But that's another story for another time.

Father Gilligan wrote some very nice things about me the following Sunday, and the whole church prayed for my speedy recovery. I sent him an autographed picture, and he replied by bringing around little Mary Alice, who was suddenly my biggest fan.

I showed her my scars, and she showed me the scab on her knee she'd received when she tripped and fell, running out of the church. She thanked me, gave me a hug around the neck, and read to me the card the kids had made.

It was a hand-drawn picture of Santa Claus holding a tiger over his head. I kept that in the bar, stuck in the corner of the big mirror, for years. I don't know if it was a mistake or someone was trying to be clever, but underneath the little drawing on the front was the name, *Santa Tom Sharkey*.

# SAILOR TOM SHARKEY - BIO

"Sailor" Tom Sharkey (1873-1953) is widely considered one of the greatest fighters of the Golden Age of Boxing. Born in Dundalk, Ireland, he joined the Merchant Marine when he was twelve years old, sailed the world, and if you believe his account of his sailing days, he was shipwrecked four times.

He landed in New York City at the age of 17 and was briefly employed as a blacksmith before he signed up for the U.S. Navy. By the time his ship had docked in Hawaii, Sharkey was eager to begin his career as a pugilist. Standing at a mere 5' 9," he cultivated one of the most formidable physiques in the sport with his bull-like neck and a 44" chest, tattooed with a four-masted schooner and the motto, *Never Give Up the Ship*.

Sharkey competed against the cream of the crop of heavyweight contenders in his time and always gave them the hardest fights of their careers. Boxing historian Tracy Callis remarked, "He had the bad luck to fight when Jim Jeffries, Bob Fitzsimmons, and Jim Corbett were around. Had he fought in any other period of history, he probably would have been a champion."

Sharkey is best remembered for his brutal and legendary 25-round fight against Heavyweight champion Jim Jeffries (the first prize fight ever filmed) and for his controversial fight against Heavyweight champion Bob Fitzsimmons, a fight refereed by none other than Wyatt Earp.

Sharkey retired from the ring in 1904, but remained a colorful public figure for the remainder of his days.

# ACKNOWLEDGEMENTS

I am indebted to a number of people who contributed to the development of Sailor Tom. I first workshopped this idea at one of the annual Clockwork Storybook retreats, and Bill Williams, Chris Roberson, Matt Sturges, and Bill Willingham were especially encouraging and instructive with their comments.

I also received a lot of interest and enthusiasm from fellow Robert E. Howard boxing fans Chris Gruber, Jeff Shanks, and Rusty Burke.

The real work on Sailor Tom Sharkey was done by boxing historian Tracy Callis and journalist Greg Lewis, whose biography, "I Fought Them All," was long overdue. Every single exaggeration made by me was completely intentional, and should not reflect at all on the research he and so many others have done.

Of course, these stories wouldn't exist at all had it not been for Robert E. Howard and his humorous prizefighting series about one Sailor Steve Costigan.

I've wanted to play in that sandbox for years, but was frankly not interested in pastiche. It took a decade or more to figure out my own voice and my own way of doing a funny boxing character, and it was in the course of all of my research on Robert E. Howard that I stumbled across the idea for using Tom Sharkey as my muse.

So, thanks to Robert E. Howard and also longtime friend and big brother John Lucas for validating with me that guy from Texas who wrote all of those sword and sorcery stories could also be funny as hell when he wanted to be.

# ABOUT THE AUTHOR

Mark Finn is over forty and has no tattoos. He lives in North Texas atop an old movie theater with his long-suffering wife, far too many books, and an affable American bull terrier named Sonya.

EVERY MONTH YOU CAN
DEPEND ON MORE
HARD-HITTING, TWO-FISTED,
FIGHT CARD ACTION!

# FIGHTCARD

GET ON
THE FIGHT CARD TEAM
NOW!

## FIGHT CARD VOLUME 1
### 2012
FELONY FISTS / THE CUTMAN
SPLIT DECISION / COUNTERPUNCH
HARD ROAD / KING OF THE OUTBACK
A MOUTH FULL OF BLOOD / TOMATO CAN COMEBACK
BLUFF CITY BRAWLER / GOLDEN GATE GLOVES
IRISH DUKES / THE KNOCKOUT

## FIGHT CARD VOLUME 2
### 2013
RUMBLE IN THE JUNGLE / AGAINST THE ROPES
THE LAST ROUND OF ARCHIE MANNIS
GET HIT, HIT BACK / BROOKLYN BEATDOWN
CAN'T MISS CONTENDER / BAREFOOT BONES
FRONT PAGE PALOOKA / SWAMP WALLOPER
FIGHT RIVER

## FIGHT CARD VOLUME 3
### 2014
MONSTER MAN / GUNS OF NOVEMBER
ADVENTURES OF SAILOR TOM SHARKEY

## FIGHT CARD MMA
WELCOME TO THE OCTAGON
THE KALAMAZOO KID / ROSIE THE RIPPER

## FIGHT CARD ROMANCE
LADIES NIGHT / LOVE ON THE ROPES

## FIGHT CARD LUCHADORES
RISE OF THE LUCHADORES

## FIGHT CARD NOW
PUNCHING PARADISE

## FIGHT CARD SHERLOCK HOLMES
WORK CAPITOL

FOR MORE INFORMATION ON

# FIGHTCARD

GO TO:
http://fightcardbooks.com

**FIGHT FICTION IS BACK!**

Printed in Great Britain
by Amazon